The Cost of Loyalty 3

Lock Down Publications and Ca$h
Presents

The Cost of Loyalty 3

A Novel by *Kweli*

Lock Down Publications
P.O. Box 870494
Mesquite, Tx 75187

Visit our website @
www.lockdownpublications.com

First Edition May 2020
Printed in the United States of America

Lock Down Publications
Like our page on Facebook: Lock Down Publications @
www.facebook.com/lockdownpublications.ldp
Cover design and layout by: **Dynasty Cover Me**
Book interior design by: **Shawn Walker**
Edited by: **Nuel Uyi**

Stay Connected with Us!

Text **LOCKDOWN** to 22828 to stay up-to-date with new releases, sneak peaks, contests and more…

Thank you.

Submission Guideline

Submit the first three chapters of your completed manuscript to ldpsubmissions@gmail.com, subject line: Your book's title. The manuscript must be in a .doc file and sent as an attachment. Document should be in Times New Roman, double spaced and in size 12 font. Also, provide your synopsis and full contact information. If sending multiple submissions, they must each be in a separate email.

Have a story but no way to send it electronically? You can still submit to LDP/Ca$h Presents. Send in the first three chapters, written or typed, of your completed manuscript to:

LDP: Submissions Dept
Po Box 870494
Mesquite, Tx 75187

DO NOT send original manuscript. Must be a duplicate.

Provide your synopsis and a cover letter containing your full contact information.

Thanks for considering LDP and Ca$h Presents.

Acknowledgements

Ca$h, thanks for having patience with me, as well as providing the platform that allows me to present my penmanship to the people. (a double salute)

To my young homie, King Doogie, I view your friendship as a blessing, 'cause you definitely enable to continue this journey as smoothly as possible. (Much Love!)

Can't forget about my lil mans, BD Twan, from 45th & Dreaxler. Stay focused and alert my G. (Up1 on the rise!)

To those who purchased my books, gratitude. Because what is an author without readers?

If monetary value was attached to shout-outs, then I'd name every single person I know. But it's not. So, I'll keep it simple and say I sincerely hope that every Real One I know or ever crossed paths with prevail.

A word from the author...

A lot of people have read my books and expressed surprise at my style of writing. I tell them all, "Acquiring an education is essential, regardless of your age or upbringing."

If you truly love and value yourself as a person, then you will ensure that no one can legitimately label you as ignorant or unintelligent.

So gas up or get left behind. PERIOD.

Kweli

INSANITY

She appealed to our eyes at an adolescent AGE and not even our mothers could convince us of her disloyal WAYS.

We swore she'd fulfill our endeavors and DREAMS as we watched her turn champs into tramps and fathers into FIENDS.

We felt safe in her presence 'cause presents were PLENTY and what should've been ugly we labeled as PRETTY.

We abandoned our families on behalf of this WHORE she was filling our plates with pain and we were begging for MORE.

Devoid of devotion she has no EMOTION yet, we continued to swim in her shark-filled OCEAN.

We'll curse and disown her when walking that YARD then once we're released, we scurry right back into her heartless ARMS.

Knowing she causes our friends to be brazenly KILLED knowing how Cheetah got life and just lost his APPEAL and knowing how Miko got miserably trapped in that chair with four WHEELS.

For those unable to decipher this message, then let me say it CANDIDLY to think that you can wife the streets and win is nothing short of INSANITY!

May the Real prevail,

Kweli.

Chapter 1

Terry Jones was forced to take a seat after Malikah blew his mind with the news that Juan-Juan was the father of her son, Booka. With the resemblance between the two undeniably strong, there was no doubt she was spewing facts.

Unable to contain her excitement, Malikah sat across from Terry and asked in an eager tone, "You knew him, didn't you?"

Slowly nodding, he looked up and answered, "Youngblood was like family."

This being a day she thought would never arrive, Malikah teared up as she pulled Booka close and gently kissed his cheek. After years of praying, she was finally being given the chance to learn about her baby's father, which was a vital piece of information she could pass along to her son.

For nearly an hour, Terry answered her profuse questions before presenting her with one of his own. "So how did y'all meet?"

Reliving the memorable night she and Juan-Juan had spent together, Malikah explained she'd been a dancer at the strip club, Onyx, when their paths crossed. ". . . And from the moment we locked eyes, I knew that young boy was official."

Malikah was the stripper known as 'Redd', whom Juan-Juan had hooked up with when he, J-Bo, and the two cats from Cleveland flew to Atlanta before doing the bank robbery. After the night was cut short on account of Ham's stupidity, Malikah had been left pregnant and with little knowledge of the man responsible for impregnating her.

While Terry and Malikah were quietly collecting their thoughts, he glanced over at Booka, who was watching him with an intensity uncommon for a five-year-old. *He's the spitting image of Juan-Juan*, Terry thought, chuckling to himself.

With their encounter now clearly on a more personal level, Terry leaned forward and addressed her with genuine concern. "No matter how hard it is, I need you to tell me exactly what's going on in your life." As a true friend of Juan-Juan's, Terry Jones would ensure that his son was safe by all means.

Intuition told her he was trustworthy, so Malikah revealed how she had fell under the spell of a hustler named Deon shortly after Booka's birth. "He'd been chasing me for so long, and one day I finally stopped running."

Despite the warnings from several of her friends, Malikah allowed Deon to move her to the outskirts of the city, where he accompanied her on frequent shopping sprees and perfectly played the stepfather role.

However, accustomed to providing for herself, she decided to return to the Onyx, and informed Deon of her decision. Once he saw he couldn't change her mind, he removed his mask to reveal the cold and manipulative monster for whom he was.

"I done gave yo' ungrateful ass everythang you could possibly wont!" he barked one night, as they stood toe-to-toe in their bedroom. "You know how many bitches would *love* to be in yo' position?"

"Well, excuse me for not being the *weak* and ambitionless bitch you want me to be, Deon," she sassily shot back. "But I been getting my own since I was a jit, and with or without yo' consent, I'ma continue to do so."

Without another word, Malikah marched to her closet and began throwing clothes into a suitcase.

"Fuck is you doing?" Deon growled, as he came and hovered over her.

"Packing only what I came with."

He grabbed her arm when she tried to step around him. "Malikah quit playing with me."

"This aint no game, Deon. I refuse to let *any* man prevent me from—"

Thwack!

The force of his backhand sent her flying back into the closet. A tigress at heart, she quickly sprung up from the floor and rushed him. But her attack was no match for a grown-ass man, and Deon manhandled her with ease and no mercy.

With one of her eyes nearly swollen shut and her lip split, she screamed at the top of her lungs as he dragged her downstairs by the hair.

"You wonna leave, then get the fuck out!" Deon shouted, as he flung her to the floor and opened the front door.

"Let me get my baby first," Malikah said, looking at him pleadingly, as Booka's wail echoed throughout the house.

"Naw. If you wonna strip, then go strip. But you ain't taking him with you."

"Deon, you know I can't leave my son."

"Well, you better decide what you gon' do. 'Cause you ain't getting both."

"Deon, please—"

"What you gon' do, Malikah?" he asked, his voice heavy with impatience, his eyes devoid of sympathy.

With no choice but to comply, she quietly answered, "I'ma stay."

On their way back upstairs, Deon grabbed the back of her neck and warned, "You know my youngins will hunt you down if I make the call, so don't even *think* about trying take yo' son and sneak off."

Staring at her battered reflection in the bathroom mirror later that night, Malikah couldn't believe the man she loved was subjecting her to imprisonment under his roof.

Terry Jones was inwardly steaming as he took in her story. He was not the type to interfere in another man's relationship, but the coward Deon definitely deserved to die.

Just when Terry thought he'd heard it all, Malikah went on to confess something much worse.

"To make sure I never left and was entirely dependent on him, he got me hooked on drugs."

She explained how Deon came into the bedroom one day with Booka in one hand, and a heroin-filled syringe in the other. Throwing the needle on the bed, he withdrew a pistol from his waistline and held it to Booka's head. "Find a vein, or I'ma blow this lil' nigga shit off."

From that day onwards, she became a slave to her supplier.

***

It wasn't until recently Malikah received the wake-up call that rung loud enough to awaken her from a drug-induced slumber.

She had gone into Booka's room one morning to horrifically find him poking a syringe at his arm. "Booka, what are you doing?" She yelled in panic, snatching the syringe from his hand.

The little boy innocently replied, "I'm just doing what I be seeing you do, momma."

Holding him in her arms while she cried like a baby, Malikah abandoned her pride and embarrassment, and reached out to one of her friends by phone. "Girl, please come get me. I can't live like this no more."

Now, after being clean for several months, here she was sitting next to Terry with the grit to get her life back on track.

Deeply touched by her revelation, Terry pulled her into a comforting embrace and promised, "As long as I have breath in my body, I will do whatever I can to support you and your son."

When Malikah's ride called to tell her that she was outside, Terry Jones wrote her a $5,000 check before walking her out to the car. "And don't worry about any furniture or appliances," he assured her along the way. "I'll have the house fully furnished by tomorrow."

"You a good man, Terry," she said, after laying a sleeping Booka in the backseat. "I can tell Juan-Juan must've meant a lot to you."

After exchanging numbers and agreeing that she would move in the following day, Malikah slid down into the turquoise-colored car and waved as it pulled off. Inwardly, she was excited about her and Booka's new home.

Walking over to a Maserati coupé, Terry opened its door, paused to look toward the sky, and made Juan-Juan a silent promise. *I'ma look after yo' seed, Youngblood . . . no matter the cost.*

Chapter 2

Atlanta

I done flew too high to crash like this, Fat-Cat reasoned to himself, as he and Shooter were in a stand-off with D-Wub and his men. So, relying on wisdom instead of weaponry, he spoke up before it was too late.

"I ain't even gon' lie to you, 'Wub. I might be *willing* to die, or even go do a bid, but I don't want to, though. Especially not over what we both know is some bullshit. We done lost enough good men, bra. So I'm saying—"

Skurrr!

Skurrr!

Skurrr!

Before Fat-Cat could finish his statement, three Dodge Demons sped into the plaza and skidded to a stop. Six hooded hooligans hopped out holding assault rifles, and stood in front of the barbershop's window. Their message was clear; regardless of what happened inside the shop, D-Wub and his men would return to Ohio in closed caskets.

"This ain't gotta unfold like this," Fat-Cat told D-Wub, who he witnessed weighing his options with wild eyes. "So don't let yo' pride rob you of all yo' accomplishments." Knowing he was dealing with a prideful man, Fat-Cat lowered his hammer and motioned for Shooter to follow suit.

D-Wub glanced at Joe-Joe and Boss, both of whom fearlessly stood beside him, then cast his glance outside at the squadron of gunmen who were eager to squeeze their triggers. While he could certainly kill Fat-Cat, it would be a suicidal move; one he wisely concluded was not worth making.

"So, what you saying?" D-Wub asked as his weapon was still extended in a steady hand. "You just gon' let us walk up out this bitch?"

Believing that beef was only good for the burger business, Fat-Cat replied, "That's exactly what I'm saying. I don't expect us to ever be friends, but as two men who made it out the mud, we can at least be respectful of each other's success."

When D-Wub lowered his gun, Fat-Cat went over to the window and motioned for his soldiers to stand down. Obediently shouldering their weapons, they jumped back inside the Demons and skirted out.

As D-Wub turned to leave, Fat-Cat called out, "Didn't y'all come to get a perfect cut?" At $50 a head, his shop was regularly attended by ball players, movie stars, and elite from all over the city.

Calling his barbers—who were visibly surprised when they entered—back to the shop, Fat-Cat instructed them to give D-Wub and his men the signature haircuts the barbershop was well known for in Ohio.

An hour later, as Fat-Cat watched the three men climb back inside the exotic foreigns, he phoned one of his henchmen, who was lurking in the parking lot.

"What's craccin'?" Blueface answered from behind the tinted windows of a Lexus Coupé.

"Until they back on a plane to Ohio, don't let 'em out of yo' sight."

D-Wub's appearance had just uncovered the grave in which Fat-Cat had buried his past. And with the enemy knowing the location to one of his most lucrative businesses, there was no way he could now avoid doing what had to be done. He refused to toy with his safety or the safety of his loved ones.

"We gotta cut buddy off at the root," he told Shooter that night before they parted ways. "But don't make a move until it's a definite checkmate."

The art of annihilation being his specialty, Shooter nodded, "Say less, Cuz."

After the strangulation of Eli, who had been the state's star witness against Shooter, the prosecution had no choice but to release a man they *knew* was a murderer. Indebted to Fat-Cat for orchestrating the whole play, Shooter agreed to become his right-hand and moved out to Atlanta. Now, four years later, he had more money than he knew what to do with, and would gladly give his life on behalf of the man responsible.

***

Later that night . . .

Pulling into the crowded parking lot of Magic City, the Wolf Pack hopped out a black Trackhawk, carrying solemn expressions on their faces. They approached the doorman and gave him one-thousand dollars with instructions to go fetch the manager.

Minutes later, they were escorted to a back room, where D-Wub sat across from the owner as Joe-Joe and Boss stood on either side of the door.

D-Wub removed a wrist-sized roll of money from his Amiri jeans and tossed it across the table. "I need you to lock this bitch down till we leave. We gon' buy every bottle you got, and throw close to a hundred."

As he considered the mathematics and took in their celebrity-like appearances, the owner nodded obligingly, "Arrangements can be made." The opportunity was too profitable to pass up.

On cue, Boss left the room and returned a minute later with a Louie backpack. He laid it on the table, unzipped it and began removing its contents. There were bricks of money, which was to be turned into singles. The bag also contained a zip of pressure and three bottles of cognac, which the owner had seen only on one other occasion.

A glutton for stunting, D-Wub ordered a slew of gold bottles as he handed the owner a limitless Black Card. "And make sho' them bitches sparkling, Blood."

Nearly packed to its capacity, the atmosphere inside Magic City was electrifying as Cardi B's hit song, "Bodak Yellow", played through the speakers. With multitudes of gumbo-thick dancers and the constant showering of loose bills, it definitely lived up to its reputation.

As a precautionary move, the Wolf Pack chose a VIP stage table. After the earlier encounter with Fat-Cat, it was imperative that they watch their surroundings.

Before going to lock the club's door, the owner spoke into a bartender's ear and pointed in D-Wub's direction. Her eyes brightened with excitement as she rushed to tell several others to accompany her to the back.

***

Attracting every eye in the building, the bartenders marched from the back with over two dozen sparklers, a tray full of money, and three bottles of Louis XIII 'Black Pearl edition', which was $13,000 a pop. It was Joe-Joe's twenty-sixth birthday and the Pack was sparing no expense.

"Girl, them bottles like twenty thousand apiece," a woman told her friend as they sat at a nearby table. "And that's gotta be at *least* a hundred thousand in singles."

While taking measured sips straight from the Louie bottles, Joe-Joe was drizzling bills over two strippers as they gave him a competitive lap dance. Lightweight was upset about their change of plans; his initial intention was to bring several strippers back to his suite and make a movie. But being in the enemy's backyard meant his lower desires were to be put on hold.

"We still gon' blow up in this bitch and show out," D-Wub had said while on their way to the club. "But we ain't dying over no pussy."

When Future's hit single 'Mask Off' came on, Joe-Joe said, "Let's get this shit popping, Blood," then stood up and began waving strippers toward their section.

Quickly vacating booths and tables, titties were bouncing and asses jiggling as women rushed to take their place on the stage. Then, amid envious stares and recording phones, the three men threw $26,000 apiece, saturating the stage with 78,000 singles.

As the money was being scooped into trash bags, they hit the Louie once more, saluted the club and turned to leave.

"Aye, hold up!" one of the dancers yelled out as she jumped down from the stage. She was willing to spend the night with any of them.

D-Wub cut her short with a firm headshake. "It's over with, ma. We got a flight to catch."

She frowned in confusion, nudged her head at their table and asked, "But what about all these bottles?"

D-Wub smirked. "Merry Christmas."

Hearing that, the two women seated at the nearby table quickly hopped up and went straight for the palladium-plated bottles of Louie. Because not only were they over halfway full, but each bottle alone was worth an easy grand.

As part of their agreement with the manager, four armed security men stood guard in the parking lot as the Wolf Pack exited the club. Handsomely rewarded for their services, they shouldered standard AR's as the Ohioans made their way to the Trackhawk.

Patiently parked across the street at the bus station was Blueface, whose hand was cupped over a cigarette to shield the glow. He followed the Jeep back to a five-star hotel, then later to Atlanta International, where the Wolf Pack soon boarded a first-class flight back to Ohio.

As the Boeing was accelerating down the runway, Blueface called Fat-Cat and informed, "They in the sky, Cuz."

Despite his heavily active role in the streets, Blueface had acted on his passion for weightlifting and purchased his own gym. In the midst of installing various exercise equipment, his long-term plan was to forsake the game and become a personal trainer. The young savage just hoped he lived long enough to make the change.

Chapter 3

Lucasville Prison

"Aye, Eddie, wake yo' soft ass up, nigga!" Moondo drunkenly yelled through the bars of his cell. "I know that hoe ain't got you down there *stressing*!" Having downed nearly a gallon of hooch, Moondo was ready to talk shit and kick it.

After a silent thirty seconds, Moondo yelled again. "Aye, *Eddie*!"

"Lay yo' drunk ass down, nigga!" someone from the lower tier spazzed. "Niggas trying to sleep."

A certified cell-warrior when drunk, this was all the fuel Moondo needed to crank up.

"Nigga, *fuck* yo' sleep!" Moondo shot back. "And if you don't like it, *bond out*, bitch ass nigga. And that go for you and whoever else that feel some type of way. You niggas got this jail shit twisted . . ."

Lying in his rack with his hands clasped behind his head, J-Bo was blankly staring at the ceiling. He was thinking how being in a place like this was similar to the case of a sane man trapped in a nuthouse. So, regardless of how hard you tried, this was an environment to which you could never adjust.

As Moondo continued his vicious barking, an old-head serving a life sentence with no chance for parole intervened. It wasn't his place, but he was fed up with the man's disrespectful behavior.

"Aye, Moondo, this Gator down here hollering at you, lil' bra."

"Nigga, I don't give a fuck *who* it is. I spray old niggas, too!"

"I ain't gone go back and forth with you, youngsta. I'm just asking you to put some respect on that shit. We trying to sleep."

"Aye, Gator!"

"Yeah?"

"Suck my *dick*, bitch ass nigga!"

After identifying the nature of his surroundings, J-Bo had adopted the militant state of mind needed to navigate through such a maddening environment. He partook in no sports, which happened to be the common cause of fights. He avoided frivolous debates and developed no close friendships. Having witnessed close associates suddenly become rivals over the simplest things, he understood that this was not the place to befriend people, regardless of how cool they might initially appear.

To keep himself occupied, he worked as a tutor in the G.E.D. class, exercised religiously, and had begun writing the book on his life and Juan-Juan's. Refusing to believe his purpose was to simply perish in prison, he decided to follow the steps of Stanley 'Tookie' Williams and leave a literary legacy attached to his name. Determined to ensure that the world remembered him long after his death, Javontae Bowden was a 'lifer' with a cause; something that enabled him to march through the madness with his back straight and head up.

It was an hour later and Moondo was still fully charged. He had moved on from Gator, who refused to engage in the verbal exchange, and was now addressing no one in particular. "I been whooping shit all my life! You bitch ass niggas better ask about Moondo!"

Tired of hearing the fool who was just a few cells away, J-Bo grabbed his JP5 player and turned the volume up until Moondo could no longer be heard. Listening to the soothing voice of Sade, he rolled toward the wall and closed his eyes.

***

A week later . . .

"*Ahhhhhh*!"

A piercing scream inside the block had everyone scrambling to the front of their cells. For those that could see, their eyes were glued to the end of the range, where a vicious display was underway.

Gripping a foot long knife, referred to as a 'Hawk', Gator had Moondo hemmed up in a corner as he repeatedly drove the piece of steel into his upper body. To ensure that the knife didn't slip from his hand, he had put a string through its handle and tied it around his wrist. And by the look in Gator's eyes as he hacked with the efficiency that came from experience, it was evident he intended to stop Moondo from breathing.

When Moondo had been cell-banging on Gator the other night, the old-head was in his cell quietly fuming. “This nigga don’t respect life,” Gator mumbled to himself as he sat on the edge of his bed with clenched fists. “He think a nigga won’t kill him.” It was then he decided he would take one for the team and tuck Moondo in. Already doing life without the chance of parole, he had nothing to lose.

The opportunity presented itself a week later when Moondo was using the phone. Speaking in a hushed tone as he and his baby mother engaged in phone sex, he had his back to the range while slyly fondling himself. Forgetful of his prior actions, he was completely caught off guard when Gator crept up behind him and drove the blade into his back.

As Moondo’s body jerked in reaction and the receiver fell from his hand, Gator yoked him up with one arm and buried the blade near his kidney. At that point, Moondo let out the first of many high-pitched screams.

“Talk that gangsta shit now!” Gator growled, as he repeatedly snatched the knife out before savagely shoving it back in.

“C.O.! C.O.!” Moondo cried out, as he tried to block the blows. With every painful puncture, he could feel his life gradually slipping away.

His face splattered in blood as he continued to hack into Moondo’s flesh, Gator was unable to hear the female’s voice screaming through the receiver. Horrifically hearing the whole ordeal, she was begging for the attacker to spare the life of her child’s father.

In full riot gear, a herd of C.O.’s blitzed the block and ordered Gator to drop the knife. His duty fulfilled, he calmly untied the string and let the hawk fall to the floor.

Quietly standing in their doorway, convicts from both tiers watched as Gator was placed in handcuffs and led out the block. While they hated to see a good man go down for the killing of a clown, they found satisfaction in knowing that his situation couldn't get much worse. Besides the temporary loss of commissary and appliances, he had basically caught a free body.

Once he was declared dead by paramedics, Moondo's mangled body was placed on a gurney and covered with a bed sheet.

Peering out of his window as the corpse was being wheeled out, J-Bo felt no sympathy for the deceased man. Having brought death upon himself, he was certain Moondo had learned a valuable lesson in his final moments.

There's a thin line between life and death.

Chapter 4

St. Vincent's Hospital

In a private room on the second floor, Dr. Laura Shepherd was helping one of her patients walk to the mirror in the bathroom. Having miraculously survived a gunshot wound to the head, they would be removing his bandages today.

"Ready?" she asked her patient with a gentle smile.

When he nodded in response, she reached up to remove the bandages, and courteously stepped back.

Taking a deep breath, Dr. Patterson looked up into the mirror, angling his head to where he could see the self-inflicted scar. Consumed with a mixture of emotions, he pinched the bridge of his nose as he tearfully lowered his head.

With no memory of the night he attempted to commit suicide, the doctors had explained that his heavy state of intoxication was likely the only reason he was still alive. When he had placed the .38 to his temple and squeezed, the recoil caused his hand to jerk upwards. So instead of lodging into his brain, the bullet had cracked the cranial plate and exited through the top of his scalp.

After several weeks of being in an induced coma, the swelling of his brain subsided and he was removed from the respirator machine. Much to everyone's delight, Dr. Patterson was expected to make a full recovery.

"You'll be allowed to go home in a week," Dr. Shepherd informed him as she helped him back to the bed. "And everyone here is hoping you'll eventually return to work."

With an impeccable track record beneath his belt, Dr. Patterson was indeed one of the top surgeons in the state. He was a bit arrogant. But it was the loss of Olivia that became a weight too heavy to shoulder. He would constantly have dreams in which she was crying out to him from an unknown place. So, already blaming himself for failing to protect his only child, he was finally brought to his knees when J-Bo's death sentence was commuted to life in prison. The man, he knew, was not only responsible for his anguish, but also refused to give him closure.

Dr. Patterson was so distraught that he cursed God for sparing the life of a murderer, while allowing his precious little girl to lie somewhere all alone, rotting in death. No longer having an appetite for life, it was then he decided to end it all.

Disbelief, guilt, anger, and shame were some of the emotions Dr. Patterson felt when he initially opened his eyes and realized he was neither in heaven nor hell. After he broke down and cried like a newborn, he eventually turned to the one person he knew was responsible for his miraculous survival—The Creator.

Praying for several straight hours, he apologized for his sinful and selfish act, begging God to have mercy on him and give ear to his prayer. "You make no mistakes, Heavenly father. I know it is only because of your will that I am still alive, which means you have a plan for me that I cannot yet see. So I'm humbly coming before you and asking that you reveal it to me. Please give me the strength and a reason to continue my journey . . ."

It wasn't until weeks later Doctor Patterson regained consciousness from the coma. In his heart of hearts, he knew he had to thank God through prayers, and he prayed as soon as he had the chance. For him, his being alive was evidence that God still had a purpose for him. Dr. Patterson was of the conviction that God alone has the final say. So, as a worker for the Most High, Patterson considered it his earthly duty to save a person's life by every means possible, regardless of their background or lack of healthcare.

While Dr. Patterson would forever mourn the loss of his wife and daughter, he now understood that sometimes it took a person to hit rock bottom before they could truly recognize the purpose of their life. So, in that moment, he decided he would carry on with a much more humbling attitude.

"Hey, Laura," he called out as she was leaving the room. When she turned to face him, he smiled, "Let everyone know I'll be returning to work as soon as possible."

Chapter 5

Cincinnati

"I wish you'd spend the night," Detective Anthony Flowers said to his young lover and colleague as she emerged from the bathroom naked.

Freshly showered, Detective McGee pulled a beater over her braless breasts. "I told you I gotta feed Pepper and take him for a walk," she said while wiggling into a pair of size four Polo jeans. "He's been cooped up in the house all day."

Flowers climbed out of bed, walked over and encircled his muscular arms around her waist. "I don't see why you bought a dog, anyway," he said, kissing her neck.

"You got all the man you need right here."

"Am I detecting a bit of jealousy?" she teasingly replied.

He grabbed her hand and placed it over his crotch. "I don't think I have a reason to be jealous."

A senior detective with the Cincinnati Police Department, Anthony Flowers was the head man in a Drug Task Force called RENU (Regional Enforcement Narcotics Unit). RENU specialized in bringing down the city's biggest drug suppliers. It was widely known for its thorough investigations and sometimes deadly takedowns. With over sixteen years in the force, Flowers had sent over two dozen dealers to state and federal prisons.

Flowers fired up a cigarette as he and detective McGee stepped outside into the chilling darkness.

"Call me as soon as you get home," he said, as she slid behind the wheel of her Mustang.

"Yes, father," she said in a joking tone, while bringing the engine to life.

Taking one last toke of nicotine before flicking it, Flowers bent down so that they were eye level. "In case you don't already know, I've developed strong feelings for you, young lady. Never in my career have I mixed business with pleasure, but with you I'm unable to help myself."

He took a deep breath before continuing. “I guess what I’m trying to say is, I’ll give you as long as you need. But I just wanna make sure we’re on the same page. You know, in terms of building something bigger than a friendship.”

Detective McGee reached out to touch his forearm affectionately. “Yes, we’re on the same page, Anthony. You have nothing to worry about. But, like I’ve explained to you before, I’ve been through a lot, so I just don’t want to rush into anything.”

Detective McGee had been with the C.P.D. for three years before being transferred to RENU. Impressed by her police work, as well as the measurements beneath her uniform, Flowers had approached her with the idea of becoming a narcotics detective. “I think you’d be a great player on the team,” he’d told her one evening at a police banquet.

Unable to believe the opportunity she was being offered in such a short period of time, she readily accepted the invitation. Under Flowers’ direct tutelage—an older man she found attractive—it was only a matter of time before they found themselves naked in the backseat of his squad car.

After saying he understood her point of view and would not rush her into anything, Flowers leaned into the car to kiss her cheek. “See you in the morning. And drive safe.”

With his hands stuffed inside the pockets of his pants, Flowers stared after her headlights until they were no longer visible. *What is she so afraid of*, he wondered to himself as he turned to go back inside.

***

Mount Washington . . .

Detective McGee pulled into her two-car garage thirty minutes later.

Once inside the house, she yelled for Pepper while deactivating the alarm. When she didn’t hear the 6-month-old puppy scratching at the basement door as usual, she instantly withdrew her Glock and listened for any sounds.

After checking the basement, which was empty, she was making her way through the living room when the hairs on back of her neck suddenly stood up. Someone was upstairs.

McGee reached down to remove her shoes, then slowly advanced toward the danger with her Glock extended. She was licensed to kill, and would do so without batting an eye.

Peering around corners the way actors often did in movies, she noticed her bedroom door was slightly ajar. Mentally preparing herself to aim with accuracy, she counted to three and spun into the room.

"Boy!" she gasped, as she lowered the gun, sighing with relief as she placed a hand over her rapidly beating heart. "I almost just shot the shit out of you!"

Wearing a smirk of amusement as he cradled Pepper in his arms, D-Wub put the dog down and walked up to September until they were only inches apart. He smelt the scent of Crest on her breath, grabbed her by the throat and shoved his tongue in her mouth.

As they hungrily sucked on each other's lips and tongues, he impatiently removed her clothes, then pinned her against the wall and gave her what Detective Flowers couldn't: back-to-back orgasms.

***

While lying in bed an hour later, September leaned up to kiss D-Wub's chin, then told him she had the information he wanted. Flowers may have been her mentor and partner, but she was currently in bed with the man she really loved and would do anything for.

Since the night they met at the club in Mt. Healthy, D-Wub and September's connection had grown to become unlike anything they'd ever experienced. The couple complemented each other so well. He had kingpin aspirations, and she was a trooper who was eager to prove her loyalty. "You lead and I'll follow, baby," she'd assured him one night. "I don't care where it is, or how deep the waters are. I'm with you."

After losing Bella and Suge, then subsequently catching the murder case, D-Wub had to go back to the drawing board and take a seat. He longed to find a way in which he could rise to the level of idolized drug lords such as Big Meech.

A scavenger for success, he soon devised a plan that would not only give him an edge over other players, but would make him one of the greatest to ever grace the game.

He first had September get a degree in criminology, then hired a strength coach to train her five days a week. Six months later she registered to become a police officer and was accepted into the academy. With her body in peak condition, she easily passed the required physical and was hired as a Cincinnati police officer.

Waiting until she had spent three years in the force, September applied for a position in the narcotics division. Already knowing the unit was led by senior detective Anthony Flowers, who had flirted with her on several occasions, she only had to wait a few months before he reached out.

Once she was made detective, September completed her role by allowing Flowers to sexually seduce her. Prying her nose wide open, she learned everything that went on in the city during pillow-talk and faithfully reported back to D-Wub, enabling him to stay a step ahead of the authorities while flooding several cities in Ohio with raw heroin.

D-Wub had taken the heroin business to such a level that every member of the Wolf Pack was now on their way to becoming a multimillionaire.

After blessing September with another set of orgasms, D-Wub rolled out of bed and got dressed.

"Be careful out there, baby," she tiredly groaned before rolling over to bury her face in the pillow.

"Likewise," he replied, wedging a full-size Glock in the front of his pants.

Pulling his hood on before leaving out through the back door, he cut across her neighbor's yard and came out on Corbily. His eyes expertly scanning the area, D-Wub slid behind the wheel of a Hellcat and sped off.

With the information September had just given him, he was about to let the dogs off the leash.

When he hit Beechmont, D-Wub cut the music up and rapped along with Moneybagg Yo:

"I think I'm the shit, big as it gets

Wrist cost a brick, I look like a

lick

Dior kicks, Chanel on my bitch

Never mind me, I'm just poppin'

my shit

Keep that stick, that's a part of

my 'fit

Championship rings, cant ball up

my fist

Two hundred on the dash, every

car that I get

Never mind me, I'm just poppin'

My shit . . ."

Chapter 6

Lebanon

Shortly before Smoke's release, he and Ghost were wordlessly blowing a joint inside a cell on the third range. Having grown close over the past three years, parting ways had them a bit emotional. With Ghost doing a life sentence, Smoke felt like he was leaving a soldier behind in an ongoing war.

"Spencer!"

Upon hearing the C.O. yell out Smoke's last name, they did a fluid Blood shake and hugged like biological brothers.

"I got you, my nigga," Smoke assured Ghost with a sincere expression. "I don't give a fuck *what* it is, just hit my line, Blood."

After his experience with prison, Smoke now fully understood the importance of having someone on the outs who wholeheartedly held it down. In most cases, a strong support system prevented the rage that resulted from frustration. The violent inmates were usually the ones without food or family.

As they were walking downstairs, where half the dayroom stood at attention, Ghost asked Smoke to have a word with D-Wub. "And tell Blood to answer his phone sometime."

Smoke nodded. "I got you, homie. But regardless of all that, I'ma *personally* make sure you straight in this bitch."

After hollering at several of his homies from Moosewood and shaking up with active members of the Blood Gang, Smoke gave a double salute, then loudly *soo-woo'd* as he bopped out the block.

Smoke's rap career had been on the brink of commercial success when he and Joe-Joe got pulled over one night as they left the club. Riding clean in a white-on-white Tesla, the envious officer said he smelled weed inside the car and called the K-9 unit. Forgetful of the fifty-six grams of heroin inside the console, Joe-Joe and Smoke felt their hearts drop when the German Shepherd started barking.

Because Joe-Joe was already a convicted felon, which meant he'd receive a harsher sentence, Smoke stepped up and took ownership. Placing loyalty over royalty, he would rather sacrifice his dream than to see his comrade catch a long bid. And regardless of what others thought, he'd make the same decision if time was reversed.

Smoke walked out the prison's front door and couldn't help but smile as he saw Joe-Joe, D-Wub, and Boss posted in the parking lot. After hugs and handshakes, the four men piled inside a pearl white Escalade.

As the ESV was floating down I-75, Smoke stripped to his boxers, then lowered the window and threw his prison clothes out onto the road. Slipping into an off-white outfit and retro Jordans, he was clasping the Wolf Pack chain around his neck when Joe-Joe tossed a fanny pack on his lap.

When Smoke unzipped it and saw the $100,000 brick of money inside, he looked over at Joe-Joe, who stated with a smile, "Welcome home, lil' bra."

***

Three hours later . . .

A mini version of Baghdad, Winton Terrace was a war zone where outsiders were unwelcome and even policemen patrolled with extreme caution. Rumored to have snipers lying on top of buildings, it was not uncommon to catch a thirty-round Glock on the waist of a twelve-year-old.

On this particularly sunny day, The 'T'—as Winton Terrace was popularly called—was alive with activities. The store on Kings Run was packed, kids of all ages were zipping through the 'hood on four wheelers, and a host of dealers were distributing heroin packs to the long line of J's parked up-and-down Winneste.

Taking this whole view all in from one of the building's stoops was Shake-D and his closest comrade, Tilla. Settled on lawn chairs with AR's within arm's reach, these were the two men responsible for the T's thriving economy.

Project babies who had been friends since elementary, Shake-D and Tilla were like night and day in appearance. Whereas Shake-D was of average height, brown-skinned and slender, Tilla was 6'5, jet-black and pudgy. But beneath the surface, both men had equally courageous hearts. With trigger fingers that constantly itched, they were the deadliest duo in Winton Terrace.

As they were on the stoop blowing a Backwoods full of pressure, the walkie talkie on Tilla's lap chirped before a voice said, "Coming yo' way."

Responding to the foot soldier with a coded command, Tilla and Shake-D were on their feet as a white SUV pulled up and parked.

Seconds later, the driver unfolded himself from the vehicle and made his way toward them.

"What's good, Fo'?" they greeted the drug lord, as he walked up on the porch.

"Big B's," D-Wub replied, then wisely declined the blunt as he accompanied them into the apartment.

Shake-D's initial plan to rob Joe-Joe and D-Wub had been cancelled on account of Tilla. Saying it would be smarter to become allies than enemies, Tilla advised him not to let his emotions interfere with his intellect. "Them niggas winning, Shake. And they need soldiers like us. So why go for some scraps when we can get a seat at the table? You feel me?"

Their chance to enlist would occur one night at a club called Celebrities. Approaching the Wolf Pack as they sat in VIP, Tilla acknowledged Joe-Joe and Boss, then asked D-Wub if he could have a word with him.

Before D-Wub could respond, Joe-Joe lifted his head at Shake-D in a questioning manner. "Wassup bra?" Recalling their last encounter, he was simply checking his pulse.

***

Shake-D swallowed his pride and replied, "My heart in the right place, Joe. I just jumped the gun, not knowing the full extent of what was going on."

D-Wub smirked. "So you the lil' nigga that was gon' try me, huh?"

"I would've done nothing less," Shake-D truthfully answered. "But like I said, I didn't know how close you and the homie was."

D-Wub hit the bottle, then got up and stood face-to-face with Shake-D. Peering into the windows of his soul, he asked him a question that would determine whether he lived to see tomorrow.

"Well, now that you know, would you still try to get me?"

With everyone tensely awaiting his response, Shake-D lifted his chin and answered from the heart, "I live by loyalty, bra, regardless of the cost. But at the same time, if you ever showed a sign of weakness, I'd be all over yo' ass. 'Cause only the strong should be in command. *Period.*"

Several suspenseful seconds ticked by before D-Wub smiled. Genuinely pleased by Shake-D's answer, it made him think of Kool-Aid—an unfit king who he had personally dethroned.

Inviting both men into the booth, D-Wub offered them a gold bottle and said the Wolf Pack was looking for new recruits. Their prayers answered, Shake-D and Tilla eagerly enlisted before toasting to a prosperous future.

As a result of Tilla's wisdom and Shake-D's courage, they were to become the pillars of Winton Terrace.

Now, several years later they were at a kitchen table with D-Wub, listening as he outlined a play he wanted them to put down. It was a deadly drill that required eight men, two of whom were pups he was sending in for what he called a 'heart-check'.

"I like these two lil' niggas," D-Wub admitted as they were walking back out on the front porch. "But if either one of 'em freeze up or get that weird look in they eyes . . . then don't hesitate."

As they watched D-Wub climb inside the Escalade and slide, Tilla looked at Shake-D and nodded, "Yeah, we definitely joined the right team."

Chapter 7

After briefly attending Smoke's welcome home party in the city, the Wolf Pack climbed inside red foreigns and got on I-75 north. Travelling with a duffel bag full of cash and a charitable spirit, they were headed to one of the most *live* strip clubs in Dayton called *Cheeks*.

Unlike most players in the game, who could not account for their wealth, each member of the Pack owned a legitimate business. D-Wub had a car lot, Joe-Joe was a real estate tycoon, Boss ran an auto detailing shop, and Smoke owned a franchised cleaning service. So while the numbers looked good on paper, it also explained their ability to ride luxury cars and throw cash around as if it was merely colored confetti.

With a 2019 Range in the lead, the five-car motorcade arrived in Dayton forty minutes later. When they curved into the club's parking lot and braked at the front entrance, they were engulfed by the familiar rush that came from stares of admiration.

D-Wub was in an R8, Boss sat low in an Aston Martin, Joe-Joe leaned right in an AMG Benz, and Smoke was gripping the wooden wheel of a Bentley coupé.

Once three licensed-to-carry shooters exited the Range and posted up like secret servicemen, the Wolf Pack emerged from their vehicles and swaggered into the club. Bypassing the line in Breitling bust downs and diamond chains, their most notable piece was the howling wolf head that glistened like a mini chandelier.

After buying out both bars and ordering buckets of champagne, they were escorted to a booth in the back that had its own private stage. When Joe-Joe opened the duffel and began stacking bricks of money onto the table, their section was instantly invaded by a flock of strippers with flawless figures.

The bartenders who delivered the sparklers were just as lewd as the dancers. Tipping them generously, Smoke settled his sights on a super-thick Puerto Rican with long hair and an olive complexion.

"Tell me what you worth for a night . . . and I'ma make it happen."

Flashing a sensual smile, she answered, "We ain't cheap."

"We?"

Nudging her head toward a dancer, who was also Puerto Rican, she replied, "Me and my girl come as a package." She then glanced down at his crotch and added, "That's if your *boy* can handle it."

If only you knew, Smoke smiled to himself before telling her to name their price.

"A thousand apiece," she stated, without batting an eye.

"Be ready in like an hour or two," he said, then lustfully watched as she strutted off with an extra twist in her hips.

As the Wolf Pack chugged champagne and threw enough money to send several students to Harvard, they were being stalked by a man from across the room. Appearing to be a boss on account of his appearance, he was actually a notorious jack boy whose clothes and jewelry were fake. Part of a three-man robbery crew, his was job was to camp out in clubs and spot potential licks. And from what he was witnessing, the men before him were worthy targets. Sending his men a brief text, he told them it was time to saddle up.

Calling it quits around 2 a.m., the Wolf Pack left the club with five females. Before pulling off, Joe-Joe collected the women's phones and said they would be returned once it was time to part ways.

They went to a Marriott on Miller Lane and purchased three suites, one of which was for the security team. "This ain't gon' take long," D-Wub informed the head man on their way into the hotel. "I'll call you when we ready."

True enough, they pressed play within minutes of entering the room.

"*Fuck*! *Fuck*! *Fuck*!" a white girl called Candy cried out, as Boss held her up in the air by the fat cheeks of her ass. Built like Iggy Azalea, she had her thick thighs wrapped around his waist as he slammed her up and down on the dick.

Joe-Joe had a chocolate stripper called Rain bent over the arm of the couch. Her ass like a jello cup, he was amazed by the amount of cum coming out of her surprisingly tight pussy. While trying to make her scream the loudest, he now understood the reason behind her name.

On the other side of the room, D-Wub had the face of a light skinned stripper mashed into the carpet as he squatted behind her and humped like a dog. Her box basic, he glanced over at Joe-Joe and asked, "What up, Blood, what that shit hitting fo'?"

"This mu'fucka *fire*!"

"Let me see," D-Wub said, as he pulled out and switched rubbers. "Cause this ain't it."

As D-Wub flipped Rain on her back and went to work, Joe-Joe grabbed the light-skinned stripper's head in both hands and started beating her mouth up. Taking it like a champ, she was loudly gagging as tears fell from her bulging eyes.

Joe-Joe looked back at Boss, who was still crushing the white girl. "Damn, nigga, let me get some of that pussy before you kill the bitch."

Fully charged off triple-stacks, they would run through a sleeve of condoms over the next hour-and-a-half.

In the suite next door, Smoke was blowing Orange Cookie while being tag-teamed by the two Puerto Ricans. As one was sucking his balls, the other was deep throating him with no hands and copious spit. His eyes rolled toward the ceiling when they both sucked a ball into their mouth and started humming together.

***

After shooting the first one on their faces and tongues, Smoke got up to put on a rubber. It was time to make them feel the effects of being sexually deprived for three years.

As both women were positioned at the edge of the bed with their backs deeply arched, Smoke had to take a moment to enjoy the visual. While the bartender was the thickest, her friend had the fattest box he had ever seen in person. *I might have to get this bitch number*, he thought, as he decided to fuck her first.

When he slid inside her glove-like gushiness, she let out a lip-biting moan and looked over her shoulder. "I need to be fucked *hard*, poppi."

Eager to oblige, he grabbed her arms for leverage, caught a rhythm, then started drilling her as hard and fast as he could. With no choice but to accept the pleasurable punishment, she was screaming loud enough to be heard by the clerk down at the front desk.

"This what the fuck you wanted!" Smoke barked, as he watched the jiggling of her soft cheeks.

As she yelled out something in Spanish, he glanced at the bartender and told her she was next. "I'ma show you what my *boy* can handle."

***

Meanwhile . . .

Across the street from the Marriott, a blue Impala was idling in the parking lot of Steak-n-Shake. Behind the car's tinted windows were three darkly clothed men with predatory expressions and stainless steel Smith & Wessons.

PJ—the passenger and unofficial crew leader—glanced at his watch for the tenth time and told the driver, Kenny, to get in position. His prediction was that the out-of-towners would be coming out shortly, so they could be back on the road before the sun rose.

Crossing Miller lane, Kenny pulled into the Marriott and parked to where he could make a hasty exit.

"One of them security niggas gotta get it," PJ voiced, as fed a slug into the chamber of his .40 and decocked it. "Cause we ain't got time to be fucking around. So the quicker we put fear in these niggas, the quicker we can get what we came fo' and get the fuck on."

"I'm with you, my nigga," Erv' readily replied from the backseat. He was the one who had been camped out in the club.

Their plan was simple. Shoot first, snatch the jewelry, then haul ass. And if everything went accordingly, they'd be splitting up $100,000 within the next few days.

"Aye, we got action!" Kenny eagerly announced, as he saw the Wolf Pack exiting the hotel's front entrance. They had allowed the women to keep the suites until check-out time and were stepping with a purpose.

Rolling ski masks down over their faces, PJ and Erv' hopped out and hurriedly crept between cars in a crouched position.

Overly anxious, Erv' jumped the gun and rose up too soon, which drew the attention of D-wub's security team.

As trained assassins, they had their weapons out within seconds.

Bdddddd! Bdddddd! Bdddddd! Bdddddd!

The hail of bullets forced PJ and Erv' to hug the ground.

Cursing to himself as he considered his next move, PJ decided he wasn't leaving empty handed and came up squeezing.

Pow! Pow! Pow! Pow! Pow! Pow! Pow! Pow! Pow!

As the two sides engaged in a steady exchange of gunfire, PJ was creeping around cars when he peeped Boss firing from onside of his Aston Martin. He aimed his .40 and squeezed twice.

Pow! Pow!

When Boss fell face forward into the car and lay motionless, PJ quickly reached down to snatch off his chains, then shot his way back toward the Impala. He encountered Erv's body along the way, but with no time to mourn the loss of his fallen comrade, he dove inside the car and yelled for Kenny to go.

Fishtailing out the parking lot as bullets shattered their back window, PJ stuck his arm out and blindly returned fire before the Impala disappeared down Benchwood and jumped on 75.

Joe-Joe was the first to find Boss, who had rolled over inside the car and was courageously clutching his cannon.

"Where you hit at?" Joe-Joe worriedly inquired, noticing his blood- soaked shirt.

D-Wub and Smoke ran up as Boss was saying he got hit twice in the back, but had managed to give one of the gunmen a headshot.

With a dead body in the parking lot and sirens growing louder by the second, D-Wub asked Boss, "What you wonna do, Blood?"

Wincing in pain, he extended his arms and said to help him up.

As they were carrying him to the Range, Boss informed them of the theft of his Wolf Pack chain.

"Don't even worry about it," D-Wub said as they laid him in the backseat. "'Cause on *blood* we gon' get that bitch back."

Telling one of the security men to take the Aston Martin, they told the other two to rush Boss to a hospital back in Cincinnati, then jumped in their own cars and fled the scene.

Listening to Boosie as he did a buck-ten in the R8, D-Wub's malicious mind had already decided on what type of example he would set when he returned to Dayton.

Chapter 8

Lucasville

"Mmmmm!" the white lady moaned into J-Bo's hand as he covered her mouth while hitting her from the back with short-fast strokes. Already two minutes in, which was pushing it, he shifted left and dug upwards. It was time to end the encounter, no matter how enjoyable it was.

While gripping the sink with both hands, her pudgy frame began to tremble from an oncoming orgasm. Several pumps later, J-Bo crossed the finish line behind her, then hurriedly flushed the condom and sent her on the way with a swat on the ass. "I'll call you tonight."

Wearing a love-struck smile, she kissed his cheek, checked her hair in the mirror, then opened the door of the staff bathroom and walked back to her classroom.

A minute later the door reopened and Pinewood-T entered the small bathroom with cleaning supplies. "Damn, nigga," he said jokingly, "It smell like a fish dinner in this mu'fucka."

After cleaning the sink and toilet, Pinewood-T stepped out and casually looked around before telling J-Bo to come out.

Thanking him for his assistance, J-Bo calmly headed back to the classroom to finish tutoring.

J-Bo met and seduced the teacher, Ms. Striker, not long after he became a tutor. Unlike others in the classroom who made desperate attempts to gain her attention, he maintained a quiet demeanor that would intrigue her more than those who were constantly in her ear.

"Mr. Bowden," she called out one day as class was ending. "Could I please have a word with you?"

Once they were alone, she continued, "I just wanted to commend you on your ability to help others become better students. It's so kind and unselfish on your part."

"Thank you, Ms. Striker. And for you to notice, that tells me a lot about you as well."

As she was blushing at the compliment, J-Bo cautiously looked toward the door. “Listen, I enjoy talking to you, but at the same time, we don’t wonna arouse no suspicion. Cause you know it’s eyes everywhere.” He then removed a piece of paper from his folder and laid it on the desk. “But I want you to read this, and tomorrow you can tell me what you think.”

It was a poem titled, *I’ve Met An Angel.*

The following day, Ms. Striker could hardly wait until class ended so that she could ask him if he knew such a woman.

“I do,” J-Bo answered as he stared directly into her vulnerable blue eyes. He sealed the deal when he added, “And every poem I write comes straight from my heart.”

From that day forward, he would feed her just enough to keep her hungry for more. Then when he was certain she was emotionally involved, he told her to get a P.O. Box in someone else’s name so that they could cancel their after-class conversations.

“The last thing I wonna do is get you in trouble, Ms. Striker. So this way, we can still have intimate talks, but without the worry of you possibly losing your job. You do understand, don’t you?”

Truly appreciative of his concern, she could only nod in response. “I’ll get it done today.”

Having her get the P.O. Box was a calculated move on J-Bo’s part. By cutting off their verbal communication, it would soon allow him to make a request she might’ve denied under normal circumstances.

True enough, Ms. Striker would begin mentioning in her letters how much she missed hearing his voice.

J-Bo waited several weeks before he presented her with a solution to their problem: bring him a cellphone.

Two days later she would nervously slip it to him after class.

To ensure that he stayed a step ahead, he quit his job as a tutor and asked Pinewood-T to get him hired as a porter in the school area. Still having no idea this was the man responsible for the permanent limp in his walk, he told J-Bo he could make it happen.

After finishing their job one day, they were walking back to the block when J-Bo asked Pinewood-T if he had ever smoked some ‘Maui Wowie’.

His eyes lighting up like a Christmas tree, he said he hadn't, but had heard about it.

"Well, you about to get the chance," J-Bo replied. "So be at yo' window tonight and we gon' blow a frog leg."

Maui Wowie was a potent strand of marijuana Ms. Striker's brother had brought back from the West Coast. Compressing several grams inside a balloon, she had hid it inside her pussy and surprised J-Bo with it during one of their bathroom encounters.

Later that day, J-Bo was at his desk working on his book and Juan-Juan's when a C.O. stopped in front of his cell. "Bowden, you got mail."

Assuming it was from his secret lover, he was surprised when he saw it was addressed by Terry Jones. When he opened the envelope and saw the small photo inside, it took only a split second to make the connection.

Ain't no way, J-Bo thought to himself in disbelief. Turning it over, he read the brief message on back that read, 'Juan-Juan's son, Booka. Five y/o.' Unable to tear his eyes away from the picture, J-Bo knew this was exactly how Juan-Juan looked when he was this same age.

Overwhelmed with emotion, J-Bo had to blink back tears as he was forced to face a heartbreaking reality. With Juan-Juan dead and him doing forever, neither of them would ever be able to physically assist this handsome little boy through life.

Chapter 9

Atlanta

Fat-Cat, Shooter, and Blueface were standing in front of a large building in Zone 6 when a black-on-black Suburban pulled into the parking lot. Seconds later, a familiar face and two other hulking figures emerged from the SUV's snow white interior.

"What's craccin?" Baby-Herc' greeted, pulling each of them into a brotherly embrace. Recently drafted into the League, Baby-Herc' was now a star running back for the Chicago Bears.

"Got-damn, Cuz," Shooter smiled, as he stepped back to size him up. "You done got even bigger. What the fuck is they feeding you?"

Despite his professional career and the signing of a thirty-million-dollar contract, Baby-Herc' had remained in close contact with his childhood friends over the years. On account of their love and support after Jinx's death, he would always say it was because of them he had been able to fulfill his dream.

A few minutes into their reunion, the football star turned his attention to the building they were standing outside of. "So this is it, huh?"

Fat-Cat nodded, "Yeah, this it."

On behalf of Jinx, as well as the desire to give back to the community, Fat-Cat had opened up two recreation centers called, 'Links From Jinx'. One in Toledo and the other here in Atlanta, they were more than just indoor playgrounds for kids to come and play at.

He offered free G.E.D. courses—where all achievers received one thousand dollars in cash. There were qualified tutors to help students with homework, janitorial jobs for teenagers who wished to earn legitimate income, and a daily raffle that paid out $250.

Because Fat-Cat knew the importance of having clean clothes for school, he spent $200,000 every year on clothes, shoes, and backpacks. So instead of simply preaching to the youth, he went a step further and actually offered them a way out.

Baby-Herc' was also a major contributor to both rec' centers. Regardless of how many yards he ran or millions he earned, he knew life could've been a lot different for him had he lacked the proper support. So when Fat-Cat approached him with the idea of building a legacy in memory of Jinx, he didn't hesitate to write him a check for $2 million.

Upon Baby-Herc' receiving his first tour of the center, where it warmed his heart to see the smiling faces of so many young ones, he pulled Fat-Cat into another strong embrace. "Cuz is definitely looking down with a big ass smile."

After signing a number of autographs and encouraging the kids to stay on the right track, it was time for Baby-Herc' to head back to the Windy City.

As they were outside exchanging hugs and goodbyes, Baby-Herc' said he had a surprise for them, then reached into the truck and grabbed a manila envelope. He handed it to Fat-Cat and said, "This season tickets to all my games."

Promising they would use some of the tickets, they gave him a double salute before he was chauffeured off toward the airport.

With Shooter and Blueface responsible for overseeing the illegitimate half of Fat-Cat's empire, they dapped him up, then hopped inside a Demon and sped off. Like the countless cadets across the nation, they were willing to risk their lives and freedom in return for fame, power, and the ability to blow money like a runny nose.

Before turning to go back inside the rec' center, Fat-Cat looked up at the sky and smiled. "We made it, my nigga."

While Jinx may not have been present physically, Fat-Cat would ensure that the memory of him forever lived on.

***

Later that night . . .

When Fat-Cat entered his six-bedroom home, he noticed a trail of rose petals that led toward the spiral staircase. Removing his jacket as he made his way upstairs, he smiled at the sight of his beautiful wife posing in the doorway of their bedroom.

Wearing a seductive expression and see-through lingerie, Kiona traced a hand over her voluptuous figure and asked, "Do you want this, baby?"

"Always," he answered, hungrily walking down toward her.

Kiona held out her hand to stop him. "Not yet, baby. I'ma first need you to get cleaned up while I finish cooking." She leaned in to passionately kiss his lips. "Then I'm all yours."

After sitting on Fat-Cat's lap and feeding him a plate of homemade meatloaf, mashed potatoes, corn, and buttermilk biscuits, Kiona got up and grabbed his hand.

"Now come join me for desert," she said before leading him upstairs.

"Damn!" Fat-Cat said to himself, as he watched the provocative jiggling of her hefty cheeks.

In their room, Kiona had him sit on their California King as she danced to Beyonce's song, 'Drunk in Love'.

Lustfully tuned in to her every move, Fat-Cat bricked-up when Kiona bent over at the waist and made her ass cheeks clap in sync with the song.

Kiona got on her knees and crawled over to the bed, kissing from his feet to his inner thighs. She moved his hand when he tried to remove his briefs. Then slowly, she licked his dick through the cotton material.

When she finally decided to free his joint from bondage, she tenderly held it in both hands and suckled it like a newborn would its mother's tit.

Bringing him right to the edge, she released him from her mouth with a soft plop and pled, "Make love to me, Chris."

For the next thirty minutes, he passionately pushed into her caramel-toned body from multiple angles.

She felt herself nearing a second orgasm and cried out, "Oh my god, baby, I'm 'bout to come again! Please come with me!

Picking up his pace as he stared down at her facial expressions and bouncing breasts, the visual was enough to get him there.

After wiping him down with a warm wash cloth, Kiona snuggled up to him and revealed, with a smile, "You're going to be a father, Chris."

Chapter 10

With Joe-Joe handling the wheel of a Plymouth Barracuda, he, D-Wub and Smoke wore solemn expressions as the muscle car rumbled up I-75. Headed back to Dayton, they were on their way to meet someone who had information on the two men responsible for the robbery and shooting of Boss.

After being rushed to an emergency room in Cincinnati, Boss was treated for the two gunshot wounds to his upper back. Once he made it out of that critical state, the doctor informed him of his close encounter with paralysis. "You should consider yourself a lucky man, Mr. Anderson. Because one of those bullets was just millimeters away from leaving you paralyzed from the neck down."

While his closest comrades rallied at his bedside, vowing revenge, Boss was inwardly beginning to question the direction of his life. *How many warnings do a nigga get before it's too late*? This was a thought that would sit at the forefront of his mind over the next several days.

Boss was released from the hospital a week later and placed on bed rest. As the Wolf Pack were keeping him company, Joe-Joe got the call they had been anxiously awaiting. "I found it," the voice said before hanging up.

While Joe-Joe suggested they send in the troops, this was an instance when D-Wub preferred to put in his own work. "These niggas came at us *directly* . . . so that's how we giving it back."

Arriving in Dayton, Joe-Joe pulled into a B.P. right off the highway and parked beside a 2019 Camaro.

The driver, a young hustler named Key-Weez, lowered his tinted window and passed D-Wub the Wolf Pack chain. Although the clasp was broken, the glaciers glistened as they did when the chain was initially purchased.

"What they charge you?" D-Wub asked out of curiosity.

"Fifty."

D-Wub looked at Joe-Joe and smiled. "Good thang them niggas don't know about jewelry." The wolf head alone had cost $100,000.

"I can handle this if you wont me to," Key-Weez volunteered. "I got niggas on standby."

D-Wub shook his head. "Nah, you good."

"You sho'?"

"Absolutely."

Key-Weez put the Camaro in drive. "A'ight, follow me then."

A risk taker by nature, Key-Weez had grabbed his life savings and got on the road when he heard how the Wolf Pack was flooding the 'Nati with China White. Praying to the game god along the way, his prayers were answered when he bumped into a female who was friends with a female that knew Joe-Joe. She charged him $2,500 for the arranging of a sit-down.

The following day, Key-Weez was eating a double-stack at Wendy's when Joe-Joe came in the restaurant and sat across from him.

"What's popping?"

Key-Weez pushed a Wendy's bag toward him. "That's every coin to my name, bra bra."

After a moment of staring into his eyes, Joe-Joe told him to go to the bathroom.

Once they were alone, Joe-Joe withdrew a small device that was used to detect wires and waved it over Key-Weez's body. Upon passing the inspection, he told him to keep his money and sent him back to Dayton with two bricks of heroin and a thirty-day deadline.

Indeed, Key-Weez had proved to be a profitable businessman.

Because Key-Weez was now regarded as a hood celebrity, there was little that happened in Dayton he wasn't informed of. So when he heard about the selling of the Wolf Pack chain, he took advantage of the chance to prove his loyalty to the plug.

Turning into the Northland Projects, Key-Weez stopped to let Joe-Joe pull alongside him. "They in forty-six."

Joe-Joe found a parking space across from the apartment and backed in. It was now a matter of patience.

***

Inside apartment forty-six, PJ and Kenny were high off the 'Tony' as they counted the money for the third time. $50,000 was the most money either of them had ever seen at once.

"This for Erv'," Kenny said, as he bent down to snort a line through his left nostril. "And this for me," he smiled, before doing another one through his right.

Now that they had the money, PJ was ready to go his own way. He and Kenny had been ducked off since the night of the incident and he was tired of the man's paranoia. He was clutching at the slightest sounds he heard, constantly checking the windows, and worriedly watching every news channel. Cocaine was the only thing keeping him sane.

PJ separated the money into three piles and slid one to Kenny. "That's you."

Kenny frowned as he looked from his pile to the other two. "Who the third one fo'?"

"Erv's baby moma," PJ answered, as he began gathering the money up. "You got fifteen, I'm giving her fifteen, and I get twenty."

"Erv's baby moma?" Kenny repeated.

"Yeah, nigga," PJ replied in irritation. "So don't get on no greedy shit. Cause all you did was drive. You ain't have to dodge none of them mu'fucking bullets, and you ain't damn sho' ain't the one stretched out."

"I'm just saying, I never knew Erv' to have a baby moma."

"Man, you know old girl that live over on . . ." As PJ was talking he smoothly slid his gun off his waist, then turned and shot Kenny in the head.

Bang! Bang!

"Ungrateful ass nigga," PJ muttered, as he scooped up Kenny's share of the money. "Now you don't get *nothing*."

PJ was lying with regard to Erv having a baby mother. And Kenny's doubtful demeanor meant he also knew it was a lie. So, with PJ foreseeing where the conversation was headed, he simply beat Kenny to the draw.

After quickly wiping down everything he might've touched, PJ peeked out the back window for anything suspicious-looking, then opened the door and stepped out.

Crack!

D-Wub hit PJ with the butt of a gun, knocking him unconscious.

***

When D-Wub had heard the report of gunshots in what seemed like the apartment they were watching, he went off instinct and immediately hopped out the car. Creeping to the backdoor, he ducked down on the side opposite the window and waited. Because, if his instincts were on point, the shooter would come running out at any minute. Which is exactly what happened.

PJ regained consciousness and instantly went into panic mode. In the front seat of his car, he was handcuffed to the steering wheel with a red rag tied over his mouth. Uselessly tugging at the cuffs, he sensed something in his peripheral and turned to look in the backseat.

"What's popping?" D-Wub calmly greeted, as if this was a normal occurrence.

Despite the pounding of his heart, PJ eyed him with his coldest stare.

Smirking in amusement, D-Wub removed the Wolf Pack chain from inside his jacket. "Since you obviously willing to die for this, then I'ma let you have it," he said, as he leaned forward and dropped the chain on PJ's lap.

Not knowing what to expect, PJ curiously watched as D-Wub grabbed something off the backseat before exiting the car. When he saw what was in his hand, he was seized by the most fearful feeling he'd ever felt.

Holding a can of gasoline, D-Wub removed the cap and started splashing it all over the backseat.

"You tried the wrong niggas, Blood," he said, as PJ was attempting to break free. "I know it wasn't personal . . . but neither is this."

D-Wub threw the empty can inside the car and reached inside his pocket for a pack of matches and a Newport. He lit his cigarette, then, while staring into PJ's eyes, tossed the match into the car.

Woosh!

As the backseat went up in flames, PJ broke both of his wrists while trying to snatch the steering wheel out the column.

This how you cremate a nigga. D-Wub smiled to himself, as the flames slithered up front and engulfed PJ's body. Despite the rag being in his mouth, he was certain P.J's screams could be heard all over Dayton.

Pulling the Barracuda up next to D-Wub, Joe-Joe leaned over to open the passenger door and barked, "Wub!"

The merciless creature snapped out of his trance, took one last look at PJ and jumped in the whip.

As they fled the scene, someone was standing in the shadows between two buildings. Having witnessed the horrific display, he knew this was a night that would forever be burned into his memory.

That nigga the devil, Key-Weez concluded to himself, as he breathed in air that was polluted by the scent of charred flesh.

Chapter 11

Meanwhile

Back in Cincinnati, Shake-D and Tilla were minutes away from blitzing a house in a 'hood called Avondale. Travelling four cars deep, they were in a Jeep Wrangler that resembled a small tank, followed by three Chargers with neon-blue strobe lights across the front windshield. As they snaked through the city's darkened streets with purpose, the convoy gave off the official impression of law enforcement.

The Wrangler made a left on Blair and came to a stop eight houses down in front of a blue two-story. Immediately hopping out in F.B.I. flak jackets and gas masks, each man had a fully-auto MP4 with a pistol holstered on their leg.

Moving in on the house like a skilled SWAT Team, Shake-D shot a canister of tear gas through the window before a linebacker-sized soldier booted in the door.

A front-line fanatic, Tilla rushed in squeezing.

Brata-tat-ta-ta-ta-ta-ta-ta-ta-ta-ta-ta-ta-ta-ta-ta-ta!

The muzzle flashes and crackling of automatic gunfire had it sounding like the 4th of July. Having rehearsed this drill a number of times in advance, they swiftly slaughtered several shooters inside the house without any casualties of their own.

After bagging up nine pounds of pressure, seventeen ounces of heroin, a brick of fentanyl and $76,000, the eight-man army climbed back into their vehicles and headed to a downtown warehouse, where they would switch cars and clothes before going to link up with D-Wub.

Get down or lay low was an unspoken rule D-Wub had been enforcing. He was making it known through a series of ordered executions that all heroin dealers in the city had three options: shop with him, change lanes, or become a memory.

But regardless of how many people submitted, or the slayings committed, there would always be one who'd test the waters; which was the cause of the deadly demonstration just put down.

With a clique full of murderers and the hunger of a warthog, Hiram was a young savage from Avondale who had declined a seat at D-Wub's table. The invitation was extended one night at a B.P.

"I know niggas who can level you up," Shake-D had stated, as they were fueling their vehicles with premium. He nudged his head at Hiram's Beamer and added, "You could turn this into a Bentley."

Bearing a strong resemblance to the late rapper Nipsey Hussle, Hiram thoughtfully stroked his muslim-like beard before replying with direct eye contact, "No direspect to you Shake', but I don't need them niggas to help me get *shit*. And for the record, I can turn this bitch into a Bentley by *tonight* if I chose to."

D-Wub had been impressed by Hiram's rebellion. He truly admired the man's courage; it reminded him of himself. But this was business, and the rules were to be enforced upon all those who opposed. So, after doing his homework—with the help of September—he orchestrated the demise of a man he now considered a rival.

***

"That nigga Hiram wasn't in there," Shake-D and Tilla informed D-Wub, as they stood on the bank of the Ohio River.

Flanked by his two pups—who had passed their heart-check—D-Wub hid his disappointment and nodded. "A'ight. But I want y'all on that nigga ass till he on a T-shirt. I don't give a fuck *who* or how many gotta die. Find him."

Promising they would, D-Wub then gave them an even bigger incentive to do so. "I got a hundred thousand if he in a coroner office by the weekend."

"Say less," Shake-D and Tilla replied in unison. For a $100,000 on top of what they had just got, there was not a rock Hiram could crawl under.

Booter was low key steaming as he watched Shake-D and Tilla turn to walk away. He had bust his gun, too, and felt it wasn't fair that they reap all the rewards. *That nigga Shake ain't run up in the house till after me,* he angrily complained to himself.

"What's popping, Blood?" D-Wub inquired, as he noticed the sour look on Booter's face.

He tried to mask his inner feelings with a smile. "I'm good, big bra."

"No you ain't," D-Wub countered with a head-shake. "So speak yo' mind."

Nervously rubbing his hands together, Booter explained, "I'm just saying, Blood, I went up in that house and put in work, too. So I just felt like you shouldn't of let them niggas keep everything, that's all. 'Cause we got some *shit* up out of there." He was referring to the drugs and money.

"You think I'ma lame, Blood?" D-Wub calmly questioned.

"Ain't no way."

"I'm saying, you think I'm unfit to lead the Pack? Like I ain't gon' make sho' everybody fed?"

His heart racing, Booter fearfully lowered his head and mumbled, "I didn't mean it like that, big homie."

"Look at me."

When Booter reluctantly lifted his head, D-Wub shot him in the face, then stood over his body and fired again.

Bang! Bang! Bang!

He then turned to Lil' Perry. "Where you stand, Blood?"

Lil' Perry nervously replied, "To the right. Morning, noon, and night."

That being the correct response, D-Wub tucked his strap and told Lil' Perry to help him throw Booter in the water.

"No matter how small the tendency is that a man shows you," D-Wub schooled Lil' Perry on their way to the car, "you can't overlook it. Because where there's *one*, there's more. It's like going in a nigga house and seeing a roach run across his ceiling. Regardless of how nice his house might look, you'd be a damn fool to think he ain't got no more roaches up in that mu'fucka."

D-Wub locked eyes with Lil' Perry over the roof of the car before they climbed in. "It's only one way to deal with roaches,

Blood. And that's to tear the whole house down. Which is what the fuck I just did with Booter."

Chapter 12

"Yesss, daddy, gimme that *dick*!" the female loudly encouraged Smoke, as he had her on the bathroom sink. With one leg over his shoulder and the other in the crook of his arm, he was biting on her neck and chest while busting her down at various speeds and angles.

Over the loud smacking sound of their colliding bodies, Smoke heard his phone ringing in the bedroom. Ignoring it at first, he thought better of it, then grabbed her by the ass cheeks and walked to his room, bouncing her up and down along the way.

He answered it on speaker. "Hello?"

"This is a prepaid call from an inmate in Ohio Correctional Institution. To accept this call, press . . ."

Smoke hit zero.

"Thank you for using Global Tel Link. Your call is now being connected."

"What's bracking, homie?" Ghost greeted in an excited tone.

"Shit. What's good with you, Bleed?"

"I'm boolin', Blood. You know how this—"

Because the phone was on speaker Ghost could hear the passionate moans of a woman. "Aye, it sound like I might be interrupting some shit, homie," Ghost said with a laugh. "My bad."

"You good, bra. Just hit me back in like a hour."

"For sho', homie. And thanks for answering."

"Always," Smoke replied before disconnecting the call.

***

Lebanon Prison . . .

As a battle-ready gang member who was originally from the Motherland, Ghost had been given the honorary position of overseeing every Blood in the institution. A fight was not fought, a drug was not bought, or a rule was not taught without it first being cleared by him.

Three deep inside a cell on the third range, Ghost and two other Blood members were currently dealing with a serious situation. One of the Y.G.'s named Chico had been accused of sneaking out the cell of a homosexual. While the accusation came from an outsider, because homosexuality was strictly forbidden in the Blood Gang, an investigation was mandatory.

"Blood, it's three hundred niggas in this block. So why would this nigga pick *you* outta all people to put on some gay shit?"

"Cause he a *bitch*, Blood, I'm telling you. You know I don't get down like that. Fuck I look like!"

Ghost turned to T-Red. "Go get that nigga, Forty, Blood. We 'bout to get to the bottom of this shit."

When they returned to the cell a minute later, Forty fearlessly stood his ground, while staring directly at Chico.

"What's popping, homie?" Ghost greeted in a no-nonsense tone.

"What's good, Ghost."

"I'm saying, Blood, this a vicious bone you putting on the homie. So I'ma need you to tell me exactly what you saw."

"Like I told T-Red," Forty began to explain without taking his eyes off Chico. "It was on some early morning shit and I was brushing my teeth. I see the fag across the range keep peeking out his cell on some weird shit. So I step back to where he can't see me. Next thing I know, the door slide open a little bit and this nigga right here pop out the cell on some quick shit and shoot up the back stairs."

"This nigga *lying*!" Chico barked, as he punched his fist into the palm of his hand.

"Fuck I gotta lie on you fo', nigga? I'm *juuging* in this bitch."

Having heard and saw enough, Ghost told Forty to step out. "I'ma slide up to yo' cell in a minute."

As soon as Forty left, Chico turned up. "I *told* you that bitch ass nigga—"

Wham!

Ghost fired on Chico as he was talking and broke his jaw. When he dropped, T-Red put him to sleep with two vicious kicks to the head.

Chico had been found guilty by his own actions. No solid man alive would allow anyone to question their manhood and not react with violence. So when Chico listened to Forty accuse him of being gay to his face and he failed to immediately attack, that was all the evidence Ghost needed.

"Send two of the lil' homies over to that fag cell," Ghost instructed T-Red, as they were walking down the range. "He gotta get off the compound, too. And tell them if he do anything other than start packing his shit up, then break his fucking face."

As T-Red went to carry out his orders, Ghost slid back down to the phone room to call Smoke. A fellow Blood member had knocked a C.O., and Ghost needed Smoke to put together a package of drugs to be smuggled in.

While waiting on the call to be connected, Ghost thought about D-Wub. It had been a minute since he spoke to the man who swore he would hold him down for life, and he wondered what he was doing in that exact moment.

Chapter 13

Covington, KY

Right over the bridge that separated Cincinnati from Kentucky, D-Wub and September were on the top floor of a five-star hotel. With her being a narcotics detective and him a drug lord, their explicit encounters usually occurred across state lines.

After a night of nakedly wrestling all over the suite, they were now lying on the floor with her head on his stomach.

"So I've been thinking," she said before lazily licking the head of his deflated dick.

Already knowing where the conversation was headed, D-Wub pinched the bridge of his nose in irritation.

"And I feel it's time for you to get out the game, bae. We've accomplished what we set out to do, and I'm ready to move on."

When he was slow to respond, she turned to face him. "Are you listening to me?"

"How can I not?"

Slowly shaking her head, September smirked, "You love them streets more than you love me, don't you?"

"Come on yo, what type of question is that?"

"An important one, De'. Because you've made way more than enough money for us to leave Cincinnati behind and start over somewhere else. And wasn't that the plan?"

"Clearly."

"Well, why do you continue to take unnecessary risks? Especially when you know this can't go on forever. If we keep playing this game, we'll eventually lose. So why not stop while we're *winning*?"

Before he could respond, she continued. "Baby, why are you so loyal to something that's only gon' hurt you in the end?"

D-Wub moved her head and got up.

September was done letting him dodge this conversation and jumped up and grabbed him.

"Would you really prefer to be in a graveyard or a jail cell with *nothing*, than to live a normal life with *everything*? And what about your Nana? Have thought about how it'll affect her if something was to happen to you and she was never able to be around you again?"

September was making every valid point there was, but the chokehold in which the streets had D-Wub was too tight for him to break loose. And because he was not willing to tap out, there was a likely chance he'd end up being put to sleep.

For the sole purpose of discontinuing the conversation, D-Wub said he would arrange a meeting with the plug. "You know I can't just up and quit, but I'll talk to him and see what's up."

"You promise?"

"I promise," he said with a straight face, even though what he'd said was a lie. "Now let me punish this pussy one more time before we dip."

Knowing she was a fiend for the glass pipe between his legs, he balled her up and gave her the sexual high that only he could provide.

An hour later D-Wub was pulling off in a tinted Escalade when September came running out the hotel's front entrance and flagged him down.

"You left your phone, bae," she said, passing it through the driver side window. Then, stepping up on the running board, she leaned in to give him a passionate kiss. "I told you I'd follow you anywhere in life, and I meant it. But let's change the direction of our journey."

As D-Wub drove out the hotel, he had no idea that the simple mistake of forgetting his phone would be the cause of his fall from grace.

Chapter 14

Atlanta

Over a glass of red wine, Terry Jones and his fiancée, Regina, were discussing the visiting arrangement between J-Bo and Booka. Since Malikah was on felony probation and wasn't an immediate family member, she could not become an approved visitor.

"Terry, I think it's the perfect opportunity for you to sit down with Javonte and lay it all out on the table," Regina suggested. At forty-years old, Regina was a successful black woman with the physique of a fitness trainer.

Terry Jones shook his head in disagreement. "He can never know who I am. I failed him in too many ways to ever expect forgiveness."

While Terry hated to withhold secrets from Regina, there were certain things in his past she was better off not knowing. And he being responsible for the death of J-Bo's mother was one.

As Regina was on the verge of volunteering to accompany Booka on the visit, her 26-year-old daughter, Heaven, entered the living room.

"I'll do it," she quietly announced, looking from Terry to her mother. She'd been eavesdropping on their conversation the entire time.

Before either of them could possibly protest, Heaven added, "I've visited family members in jail before, Ma, so you know I know what to expect. And I'm good with kids, so Booka would definitely be comfortable around me."

Regina considered it for a moment before turning to Terry. "What do you think, baby?"

From the eagerness in Heaven's spiel and the silent pleading of her eyes, Terry knew sending her would be the wiser move. He didn't know when, but Heaven had somehow become intrigued with Booka, which likely meant that she would have his best interests at heart. And he also knew J-Bo would be pleased by her angelic appearance.

Before giving his approval, Terry Jones warned her. "Understand that if you decide to do this, it may become a monthly ritual, or however often he wishes to see that little boy."

Heaven nodded. "I understand."

Terry shot her a wink, then turned to Regina and said, "I think she'd be better company for Javonte than either of us."

Later that night, Heaven was on the phone with her best friend when she whispered in an excited tone, "Girl, I'm going to see him!"

Heaven had indeed developed a secret crush on J-Bo. She had read every newspaper article and stared at every photograph ever taken of him. And now that the chance to actually see him in person had arose, she couldn't wait to book her flight to Ohio.

***

Three weeks later . . .

J-Bo felt a mixture of nervousness and excitement as he was in his cell preparing for his visit. There were certain things that could uplift a man's spirit in prison, and being in the presence of Juan-Juan's son would definitely be a source of joy. He just prayed that Booka took to him in the few short hours they spent together.

With razor-sharp creases and a dab of scented oil, J-Bo was escorted by a C.O. to the visiting room. After handing his inmate I.D. to the visiting room officer, he turned toward the visitors and was caught off guard by something he would've never expected.

Booka was watching him, and continued to do so as J-Bo made his way over to the table and sat down.

Briefly taking his eyes off Booka, J-Bo extended his hand to Heaven. "It's nice to meet you. And again, I genuinely appreciate you doing this."

Accepting his hand with a belly full of butterflies, she smiled, "The pleasure is all mine."

While J-Bo knew he was seated across from the prettiest woman in the room, he returned his attention to Booka, who was well dressed in a Polo outfit and matching Le'Brons.

"What's up, lil' man?"

He slightly lifted his head in acknowledgement.

This Juan-Juan twin, J-Bo thought to himself in amazement.

"He's very quiet," Heaven explained, as she ran a hand over Booka's freshly twisted braids.

Just like his daddy, J-Bo further noted.

As he and Booka maintained eye contact, J-Bo leaned forward and said in his most sincere tone, "I don't know what you've been through or who you've been around with, but I can tell that you are a very smart and brave little man. Am I right?"

Booka nodded.

"How old are you?"

He stared at J-Bo for a minute before quietly answering, "Five."

"Booka, I know you don't know me like that, but I need you to trust me. You know why?"

He slowly shook his head.

"Because it's what your daddy would want you to do."

The statement caused something to flash in Booka's eyes before he asked, "You know my daddy?"

"I promise you I did."

"How?"

"Cause he was my brother."

For the first time during the visit, Booka took his eyes off J-Bo and stared down at his lap.

Not knowing what to say or what was going through the little boy's mind, J-Bo was surprised when he suddenly looked up and asked, "Was my daddy tough?"

J-Bo smiled at the understatement. "Yeah, he was definitely tough. And you know what else?"

"What?"

"He would've loved you a whole lot, too. 'Cause you exactly what he was missing in his life."

Despite Juan-Juan appearing to be incapable of having emotions, J-Bo knew with certainty that he would have loved his son. Which made him wonder why God had not arranged for their paths to cross.

***

After asking Heaven if she would get them something from the vending machine, J-Bo asked Booka what he wanted.

"Hot Cheetos," he answered without hesitation.

J-Bo burst out laughing.

Booka frowned. "What's so funny?"

"Naw, it's just that them was Juan-Juan's favorite chips, too."

"Who is Juan-Juan?"

"That was yo' daddy's name. Well, actually it was De'Juan, but everybody called him Juan-Juan. Speaking of which, what's your name?"

Booka blew his mind when he answered, "Marjuan."

Malikah had literally fallen in love with Juan-Juan during their brief encounter. So when she learned of her pregnancy, she decided to name the baby something similar to whatever Juan-Juan's real name could be. Hoping that if their paths ever crossed again, he would be proud of her decision.

As J-Bo and Booka continued to bond, Heaven quietly observed them in amazement. She couldn't believe the same little boy who had barely spoken to her during the flight was now engaged in a full blown conversation. And that J-Bo had even managed to get a smile out of him. She saw their instant connection as a sign that this convicted murderer was indeed a sincere person at heart.

When the C.O. made the dreadful announcement that visiting hours were over, J-Bo rose from the table and looked down at Booka.

"You know what would make Juan-Juan real happy?"

"What?" he asked in eagerness.

"If you gave uncle J-Bo a hug."

He felt his heart melt when Booka came forward with his arms out.

Picking him up, J-Bo hugged him tightly and breathed in his child-like scent. "You can trust me, Booka," he whispered into his ear, "And you should know that I'll always love you as if I was Juan-Juan himself."

After reluctantly letting him down, J-Bo turned to Heaven and reached for her hand. "I apologize for not including you in our conversation, but I swear I appreciate you to the *fullest*."

Flattered by his thoughtfulness, she blushed, "It's OK, Javonte. I'm just glad that you were able to get him to open up."

With lustrous dark hair, pouty lips, and a skin tone the color of sand, Heaven was the product of an African American mother and a Hispanic father. And despite her being clothed in a conservative manner, there was no way to hide the voluptuous figure beneath her pantsuit.

After she promised to return in two weeks, J-Bo leaned in to kiss her cheek. "I'm already looking forward to it. And check Booka's pocket when y'all get in the car."

During their hug, he had slipped him a picture of Juan-Juan. It was from a photo album he had had in his possession on the night of his arrest.

As J-Bo was watching them leave the visiting room, Booka brought tears to his eyes when he suddenly turned around and waved. "Bye, uncle J-Bo!"

Unashamed of his tears, J-Bo waved back. "Bye, lil' man."

While lying in his bed later that night, continuously replaying the visit with Booka, J-Bo recalled a promise he had made Juan-Juan shortly after their sixteenth birthday.

Chapter 15

2008

"It's time to level up, my nigga," J-Bo told Juan-Juan as they were parked across the street from a crowded B.P. "Cause the risks ain't worth the reward with this burglary shit we doing."

Juan-Juan nodded. With J-Bo being the thinker in their relationship, he would stand behind and enforce whatever decision he made.

Nudging his head toward the gas station, J-Bo said, "You see buddy sitting on the hood of that Charger?"

When Juan-Juan nodded, J-Bo continued, "That's Randy Bell. He gotta weed house over on Belmont, and he a easy ass lick."

A week later they caught Randy Bell coming out of the house at one in the morning.

"You know what it is!" J-Bo barked, as he and Juan-Juan jumped out the bushes with 30-round Glocks.

Randy Bell quickly threw his hands up in surrender. "Don't shoot me. You can have this lil' shit."

"Strip, nigga, J-bo ordered.

"Strip? Man, it's freezing out here."

"It's even colder in a mortuary," Juan-Juan icily warned him. "Now do what the fuck he told you."

After he lowered his pants and pulled a Crown Royal bag from out of his boxers, J-Bo opened it to look inside, then told Juan-Juan they should go, and J-Bo took off running

Juan-Juan's hesitation to move caused Randy Bell to start pleading, "Come on man, I gave it up."

Craving the euphoric feeling he got from a kill, Juan-Juan pulled the trigger.

Bang! Bang!

As Randy fell lifelessly to the ground, toes-up, Juan-Juan stood over him and unflinchingly fired several more shots.

Bang! Bang! Bang! Bang! Bang!

Staring down in fascination, he committed the gruesome visual to memory before jogging off.

Behind the wheel of a stolen Ford Tempo, J-Bo was forcing himself to stay calm as he put distance between them and the murder scene. He didn't speak until they made a left on Nebraska and were headed back to the projects.

"I would never go against you, my nigga," he said, eyeing Juan-Juan. "But was that really necessary?"

Juan-Juan nodded. "Cause now we ain't gotta look over our shoulders."

J-Bo just shook his head and smirked at the ridiculousness of what Juan-Juan just said, for they had been wearing masks after all.

When they got home, J-Bo jammed a butter knife in the door of their bedroom before pouring the money out on the floor.

Counting it several times, they couldn't believe how much it was.

"This seven bands!" J-Bo said excitedly.

Because this was more money than they'd ever seen, they would officially graduate from B & E's to armed robbers.

"So what you gone do with yo' half?" J-Bo asked Juan-Juan, thinking of the many ways in which he would spend his.

His answer not been what J-Bo had expected, Juan-Juan said, "I'm taking it back to St. Mary's."

The next day, Juan-Juan and J-Bo drove up to the orphanage in a small U-Haul.

When Ms. Teresa heard the two boys she had once split up were at the front desk seeking permission to pass out gifts, she hurried down the hall.

"Without a receipt you cannot donate anything to the children here at St. Mary's," she said as she walked up, rudely interrupting a conversation between J-Bo and another staff member.

Stifling a smile as he reached into his pocket, J-Bo withdrew a receipt from Toys 'R' Us and handed it to her. He watched in satisfaction as she studied the time, date, and amount spent.

"Where did you get the money to purchase all this?" she spat, shoving the receipt back at J-Bo.

"Teresa, may I have a word with you?" an older white lady named Ms. Catherine requested. Also a senior staff member, she remembered Juan-Juan and J-Bo from their stay at the orphanage.

A few minutes later, Ms. Catherine returned alone. "I think the children will enjoy whatever gifts you have," she informed them with a smile.

After placing everything in the gymnasium, Juan-Juan and J-Bo stood off to the side and watched as the children entered the room and noisily began claiming gifts. With over $3,000 spent, there was everything from video games to bicycles.

As Juan-Juan quietly observed the children, it genuinely pleased him to see the joy on their faces. But sadly, he knew the gifts would only temporarily brighten the gloomy situation they had to endure on a daily basis.

During a silent ride back home, J-Bo could see that something was bothering Juan-Juan.

"What up, my nigga? What you thinking about?"

"I need you to promise me something?"

J-Bo briefly took his eyes off the road. "Anything, my nigga."

"If I ever have a child and I'm not around, promise me you won't let them end up in a place like St. Mary's."

Their friendship based on love, loyalty and trust, J-Bo readily replied. "I promise to always be my brother's keeper."

Chapter 16

Toledo

After informing her parents of her pregnancy—and they were ecstatic about the idea of becoming grandparents— Kiona's father demanded that she be on the next thing smoking to Toledo. A true daddy's girl, she booked a first-class flight for herself and Fat-Cat the following weekend.

Despite the fact that he regularly revisited his hometown, Fat-Cat was still amazed by the number of scenery changes he noticed as Kiona steered them through the city in a rental. Another high school had been rebuilt; a flower-embedded divider was now on Dorr Street, and a few more black-owned businesses occupied lots that were once vacant.

When Kiona pulled into the circular driveway of her parents' mini mansion out in Ottawa Hills, Freddie and Denise Coleman were already standing outside.

"Ki-Ki!" her mother exclaimed, as she ran down toward the car to hug her only child.

Freddie—who was a bit more reserved—waited for his daughter to approach him before extending his arms with a proud smile. "My baby girl."

As the two embraced, he whispered in her ear, "Is he behaving?" This was a frequently asked question in regards to Fat-Cat's treatment of her.

Kiona leaned back to look him the eyes and assured, "I promise, daddy."

"So how long are you staying?" her mother inquired, as they were going into the house.

"Just for the weekend," Kiona answered. "I'm about to open up another clothing store, and I need to get everything situated before I'm six months. Because Chris and I have decided it would be best if I didn't work beyond that point."

While they were disappointed by the news of her short stay, her parents were at least appreciative of the precautions she was taking in regards to their future grandchild.

Once inside the house, the men were left alone as Kiona and her mother drifted upstairs for gossip and girl talk.

"Let's grab a beer," Freddie said before leading Fat-Cat into a large gourmet-style kitchen.

Average height with a permanent scowl and the posture of a Marine, Freddie Coleman was as raw as they came. Born and bred on the south side of Chicago, he had successfully fought through numerous adversities and felt no sympathy toward a weak man.

"So how's life been treating you?" Freddie asked Fat-Cat, as he opened two beers and handed him one.

"I can't complain," Fat-Cat answered before taking a sip. "Business is good and, more importantly, I can see the positive effect the rec' centers are having on the youth. Because at the end of the day, saving them is what really counts."

Freddie nodded in agreement. "Yeah, I was just reading an article in the Blade that mentioned the center here in Toledo as being a place where people can actually better themselves. So I definitely commend you on what you're doing for the community."

As Freddie was on the verge of taking Fat-Cat for a stroll out back, where he intended to steer the conversation into deeper waters, Kiona came racing into the kitchen and grabbed her husband's hand.

"Daddy, I need to borrow Chris for a second," she said before dragging him back upstairs.

The next two days flew past. It was time for Kiona and Fat-Cat to head back home.

Before they left for the airport, Freddie pulled Fat-Cat aside. "Let me have a word with you." While he didn't believe in lecturing a grown man, he did believe some men were worthy of enlightenment, especially one that happened to be his son-in-law.

As they stood out front, Freddie began, "At the time of Kiona's birth I was getting 'em straight from the plug, so you can imagine the numbers I was seeing. I'm pushing the biggest Benz, gotta team of war-ready rebels, and not to mention the level of respect attached to my name. Besides eternal life, I had it all."

Freddie paused for a split second, then continued. "I remember coming home one night and the front door to my house was wide open. I can't explain the panic I felt when I ran inside and found Denise and Kiona missing. I knew it was a kidnapping, so me and my closest men were huddled around the phone, waiting on the ransom call."

"Two days went by without a word. After blaming everything but myself, I was then trying to bargain with God, telling Him I'd change my ways if He returned my family. I had been through a lot in life, but nothing as painful as the thought of never seeing my wife and daughter again."

"Then, on the third day, Denise came waltzing through the front door with Kiona in one arm and a travel bag in the other. As I'm checking them for any signs of harm, she tell me they good and had been in a hotel for the past three days. I'm so relieved that I can't even get mad. But I did ask her why she would worry me like that."

"My wife said that the worry and heartache I felt for those three days is what she feels *everyday*. She said that because of my lifestyle, when I leave home, she never knows if I'll make it back or not. And that this was her way of showing me how she feels and what she goes through on a daily basis."

Freddie went on to add that it was then he came to his senses. He had been placing the streets before his family, which was a clear contradiction to the caliber of a man he attested to be. "How could I claim to be a man of integrity when I wasn't even putting my own family first! Which is what a *real man* does."

Freddie turned to stare Fat-Cat directly in his eyes. "Regardless of how much money you have, no man alive can be a good father from a prison cell. So don't possibly become someone who wishes he would've done it different. Because I can personally assure you, there is nothing in life heavier than the weight of regret."

Chapter 17

St. Vincent's Hospital

"Her blood pressure's ninety-over-palp'!"

"Give her two packs of lactated ringers!" Dr. Patterson said while assessing for a pelvic fracture, which could mean internal bleeding.

The victim of a hit-and-run, a twelve-year-old girl was lying on the operating table, barely clinging to life. She'd been chasing after her dog when she was struck by the driver of an F-150. Too cowardly to face the consequences of his drunken behavior, the driver had sped off without so much as a glance in his rearview.

"Cross-and-type for blood ASAP!" Dr. Patterson ordered after discovering an abdominal injury. The patient would likely have to undergo a blood transfusion.

"She's starting to decompensate!" a nurse called out, as she glanced up at the monitor.

"Push a milligram of Lidocaine and Mag'!" Dr. Patterson said, then told another nurse to administer chest compressions.

"She's going into V-Tach!"

Dr. Patterson hesitated only a split second before making his next decision. "Charge up the defibrillator to a hundred joules!" He would do everything possible to prevent this child's family from further grief.

With the paddles in hand, Dr. Patterson applied them to the girl's chest cavity and asked, "All clear?"

"Clear!" answered the nurses, who had stepped back from the table.

He squeezed the trigger.

Pop!

Her body jerked from the jolt of electricity, then lay back still.

"Rhythm still abnormal, doc."

"Increase joules to three-sixty."

Dr. Patterson took a deep breath, reapplied the paddles and squeezed.

Pop!

The body jerked, then the beeping sound of a steady heartbeat suddenly filled the room.

Amid the joyful cries of victory, one of the nurses announced, "Patient back to normal sinus rhythm. Blood pressure stabilized, one-fifteen over seventy."

"Continue to bag and get her up to ICU," Dr. Patterson said before he glanced upwards and offered a silent prayer of gratitude.

After receiving congratulatory pats on the back for his heroism, Dr. Patterson went to inform the parents that their little girl was now in stable condition.

Since his return to work, Dr. Patterson operated with a renewed energy and full faith in the Most High. Even his co-workers noticed the difference in his demeanor. While he would always long for the presence of his late wife and daughter, he had vowed to humbly carry out his earthly duties until they were reunited in Heaven.

And after much prayer and meditation, he had come to the understanding that God cannot forgive those who fail to forgive others. So, he eventually found it in himself to forgive the man responsible for the loss of his beloved Olivia.

Chapter 18

2 a.m. in Cincinnati

Bobbing their heads to the murderous lyrics of N.B.A YoungBoy, Hiram and two of his men were headed to Winton Terrace in a blue minivan. Despite knowing he was the target of an intensive manhunt, revenge was a duty he refused to forsake.

With word on the streets being that Shake-D and Tilla were offering $25,000 for information on his whereabouts, Hiram had been changing rentals and locations every three days. Refusing to flee the city, his prideful plan was to defeat the Wolf Pack one murder at a time, or until they respected his savagery enough to wave the white flag. Too cocky for his own good, he was leading his soldiers into a war where the chances of victory were virtually impossible.

The passenger inside the minivan muted the music moments before they turned onto Winneste. They were now officially in the heart of the 'T', where the price of a slip up could cost you your life.

Clutching fully-auto Macs with 50-round drums, Hiram and the passenger, Pacman, were scanning the darkened projects for any signs of movement. They simultaneously spotted a lone figure posted on one of the building's stoops.

Turning the van around, the driver, Kilo, parked on Winneste and killed the lights.

"Pull up to Shortcraft when you hear the music start playing," Hiram told Kilo before he and Pacman pulled hoods over their heads and hopped out. Quickly crossing the street, they crept between two buildings and dissolved into the darkness.

Standing on the building's stoop was a beloved native of the 'T' named Rum. He was thirstily trying to convince the female behind the screen door to let him come in.

"Rum, I aint trying to have to whoop yo' psychotic-ass baby moma."

"She ain't gon' know."

"Trust me, if I give you some of this pussy she definitely gon' know. 'Cause you ain't gone be able to stop sniffing at this door."

Rum shot her look of disbelief. "Man, that mu'fucka aint fire like that."

"Boy, this shit like drowning in hell."

With her hot-box bulging between bronze-colored thighs, Rum told her to turn around. "Let me see that fat ass."

When she turned and shifted her weight to one side, her ass cheeks jiggled enticingly inside the terry cloth boy shorts.

Lustfully gripping himself through his jeans, Rum was on the verge of offering to pay for it when the female suddenly stared past him with a terrified expression. He instantly knew someone was behind him.

Damn! was the last thought he had before Hiram and Pacman started squeezing.

Brata-tat-ta-ta-ta-ta-ta-ta-ta-ta-ta-ta-ta-ta-ta-ta-ta!

As the barrage of bullets butchered his body from head to heels, the female inside the house caught several strays as she scrambled toward the kitchen.

When Kilo sped up to Shortcraft and slammed on the brakes, Hiram and Pacman ceased fire and turned to run back to the van.

They were a first-down from safety when an unseen sniper opened fire.

Tat-Tat-Tat-Tat-Tat-Tat-Tat-Tat-Tat!

Literally lifted off his feet, Pacman was dismembered by slugs the size of AA batteries.

Barely making it to van as the sniper continued to squeeze from the roof of a building, Hiram dove in the backseat and yelled for Kilo to go. When the van began to coast, he looked up and saw Kilo slumped over the wheel. Quickly hopping up front, Hiram pushed the body out onto the street, got behind the wheel and smashed out.

Bang! Bang! Bang! Bang! Bang! Bang! Bang! Bang! Bang!

Planted in the middle of the street, two more gunmen were dumping at the minivan as it flew down Winneste before making a right on Kings Run and disappearing out of sight.

While the sniper on the roof was gathering up spent shell casings, the other two gunmen jogged to the building on Shortcraft. Walking up to the body that lay face down in a pool of blood, they turned it over and almost threw up when they saw who it was.

As one of them heatedly marched over to Pacman and Kilo and fed them the rest of his clip, the other bent down to close Rum's lifeless eyes.

"This nigga gon' act a fool", he said to himself, as he turned away from the corpse of Shake-D's 17-year-old brother.

Chapter 19

L.A.X.

An armored Escalade was idling at the airport when D-Wub stepped off the private jet. Climbing into its backseat, he settled next to an Asian assassin whose eyes were obscured behind mirrored lenses.

After passing a small wand over D-Wub's body, the assassin had him cover his eyes with a blindfold, then barked something in Chinese and the SUV was put in drive. They were headed to a meeting with the notorious Triad leader, Mr. Lee.

D-Wub didn't initially know what to expect when Mr. Lee had summoned him out to L.A. But because he'd never been late on a payment and September assured him that no one in his circle was a rat, he boarded the plane with full confidence that he'd be returning to Ohio in an even more prominent position.

Three armed guards were standing at attention when the Escalade pulled into the back of a Yokohama tire factory. With the blindfold still intact, they led D-Wub inside, where Mr. Lee and another man were waiting in a small room.

When the blindfold was removed, D-Wub showed no emotion at what he saw set up in the room. On a metal table with a chair beside it was a state-of-the-art polygraph machine.

"Will this be a problem?" Mr. Lee questioned with an intense stare.

In response, D-Wub walked over to the table and took a seat. "Hook this lil' shit up."

Once everything was in place, he was told to give only 'Yes or No' answers, then was asked only three questions.

"Are you currently co-operating with any law enforcement agency?"

"No."

"Have you ever co-operated with any law enforcement agency?"

"No."

"Do you know anyone co-operating with any law enforcement agency?"

"No."

After quietly conferring with the polygraph expert, Mr. Lee came to stand before D-Wub and extended his hand. "Three for three."

His handshake firm, D-Wub replied, "If me snitching meant saving my granny's life . . . then I guess I'd be attending her funeral."

Pleased by his solidity, Mr. Lee placed a hand on his shoulder. "Come on, I wonna show you something."

Entering a garage part of the building, two Asians were standing over a kneeling man who had been stripped down to his boxers. With a pillowcase over his head and both hands tied behind his back, he was shamelessly whimpering like a sick puppy.

"His results were not as fortunate as yours," Mr. Lee casually stated before giving his henchmen a single nod.

Dragging him over to a long work table, one of them removed the pillowcase to reveal a heavily-tatted man with thick dreads. A pleading look in his eyes as he stared in Mr. Lee's direction, he was mumbling incoherently through the handkerchief stuffed inside his mouth.

"Marco here decided he was more afraid of prison than me," Mr. Lee informed D-Wub, as he coldly returned the man's stare. "So I have no choice but to teach him the error in his judgment."

A bare-chested Asian built like Bolo Yeung suddenly soldiered into the room, loudly cracking his knuckles. He stepped behind Marco, drew his arm back and delivered a vicious body shot that made him have a bowel movement.

As D-Wub covered his nose from the stench of feces, the muscular Asian turned to face him, his different-colored eyes gleaming with excitement.

Unaffected by the odor, the Asian had the other two men lifted Marco up. The Asian then placed his head inside a large vise and tightened it enough to where he couldn't move. Telling the two men to step back, the Asian applied a strong grip on the handle of the vise and began to forcefully turn it.

The pain unimaginable, Marco screamed as the clamps were slowly crushing his skull. As the pressure increased, his bulging eyes popped out of his head and rolled on the table like small marbles.

The Asian paused to let out a hyena-like cackle, then resumed to forcefully winding the handle until Marco's head exploded like a watermelon.

Before sending D-Wub back to the airport, Mr. Lee offered him the chance to advance his position in the drug trade.

"With Marco no longer with us, I was wondering if you would like to attach his monthly shipment to yours."

This being the chance to change the direction of his journey, D-Wub disregarded September's advice and eagerly replied, "I would love nothing more."

Chapter 20

A week later

In Carhartt overhauls and leather gloves, D-Wub and Joe-Joe were standing outside a warehouse in Cincinnati when an 18-wheeler rolled into the lot. They guided the driver into the building and quickly lowered the door.

Two white men hopped out the semi and began moving with systematic speed. They used an electric siphon to drain the fuel from the semi's two modified 150-gallon saddle tanks in order to relieve the weight. Then they slid floor jacks beneath them and removed the T-Bolts with an air gun.

Quickly switching the two tanks with replacements provided by D-Wub, they filled them with the fuel from the first two tanks, reconnected the fuel lines and cranked the motor. When it didn't catch after thirty seconds, the driver cut the truck off.

Clutching a Springfield XD, D-Wub went up to the semi and knocked on the driver's door with the butt of his gun.

He cracked the door open, looked down at D-Wub and the gun, then calmly assured him, "This happens occasionally, don't panic. I just gotta let the starter cool for two minutes and try again."

After a tense two minutes, the driver cranked it again and the powerful I.S.X. motor rumbled to life.

As soon as the semi was gone, D-Wub and Joe-Joe loaded the tanks in separate vans and took separate routes to a duck-off in Lincoln Heights.

Arriving within minutes of each other, they carried the tanks into the basement and used an electric saw to cut them open. Inside, a metal divider had been horizontally welded across the middle. So, while the top halves were used for fuel, the bottom halves held 50 bricks of pure heroin. Then, as an added precaution, anti-siphon guards had been installed to prevent law enforcement from measuring the depth of the tanks.

"The whole Pack 'bout to touch a 'M' now," D-Wub boasted, while stacking bricks inside a duffel bag. Then, paraphrasing the words of Yo Gotti, he sang, "Guess God answered our prayers."

Aside from the nervousness Joe-Joe felt while being in the presence of enough heroin to get him life in the Feds, he was also feeling as if he was trapped in a pit of quicksand; gradually sinking deeper and deeper. And while loyalty would not allow him to forsake the man responsible for changing his life, he couldn't help but wonder how much longer it would be before he was swallowed whole.

***

In the backyard of his home out in Hyde Park, Joe-Joe and his thirteen-year-old son, Quran, were engaged in an aggressive game of one-on-one. The score was tied at fifteen, and the next one to score a point would be the winner.

"You better back up some, dad," a shirtless Quran warned, as he dribbled between his legs at the top of the key. "Or I'ma blow right past you."

Joe-Joe dismissively waved him off. "Just make yo' move, lil' nigga."

The leading scorer for his Junior High School team, Quran was a gifted point-guard who had aspirations of going to the league. He idolized no player in particular, but studied footages of Le'Bron the way a devout Christian would peruse the Holy Bible.

While staring into Joe-Joe's eyes, Quran feigned as if he was going left, hesitated for a split second, then gracefully crossed him over and blew past.

Chasing him down the way Le'Bron did in the finals against Golden State, Joe-Joe caught Quran as he was going up for what he thought was an easy lay-up and pent the ball on the glass.

"Get that shit outta here, lil' nigga!"

While Joe-Joe definitely didn't make it easy, he eventually allowed Quran to win the game.

Breathing heavily as they sat in the grass drinking bottled water, Quran turned to his father and asked, "Dad, why you always play me so hard?"

"'Cause I don't *ever* want you to think becoming a champion is easy. 'Cause it ain't. So whether it's basketball or just life in general, you gotta be able to play through the fouls and adversities."

Testing him, Joe-Joe asked, "Cause yo' don't want to be good as Le'Bron?"

Quran instantly shook his head and replied, "Nah, I wonna be better."

Yo muthafucking right, Joe-Joe smiled to himself.

"But you know, in order to be the best, you gotta train harder than the rest. 'Cause Curry ain't get the purest three in the league by not practising. When other people was out kicking it, you can believe that nigga was somewhere in a gym shooting threes. So always remember, Quran, self-discipline is one of the keys to greatness."

***

As Joe-Joe continued to drop jewels, the young lad felt like a sponge, soaking up everything his dad was spilling.

Despite his full-time employment with the streets, Joe-Joe was unlike the many men who allowed their children to go through life without the tutelage of a father. Personally knowing the damaging effects that resulted from a father's neglect, he had been there for his son since day one.

In fact, his belief in fatherhood was how he measured the character of a man who also had children. Because any man who does not properly provide for his own offspring cannot possibly have genuine love for anyone else. That type of character flaw is a clear indication that such a man is only out for himself.

Later that evening, Joe-Joe drove across the bridge into Covington, Kentucky, to drop Quran off at home. After parting ways several years ago, his baby mother, Crystal, agreed they could co-parent without involving the courts. And out of respect for her decision, Joe-Joe not only included her in his son's monthly allowance, but had moved them into the fully furnished condo and gave her the deed.

"You coming in?" Quran asked in a hopeful tone when they pulled up to the house. In hopes that his parents would reunite, he always tried to get them around each other.

"Nah, not today, youngin'. But tell yo' moma I said hi."

Inwardly disappointed, Quran nodded, "A'ight, I will."

He was reaching for the door handle when he suddenly remembered something and turned. "Aye, dad, don't forget we play the Tigers next week." This was a rival game he'd been anticipating all year.

"I'll be in the front row," Joe-Joe assured him.

As Quran was walking up to the house, where Crystal stood in the doorway, Joe-Joe got out the car and called for him.

"Aye, hold up, you forgot something," he said while walking toward the trunk.

When Quran came back to car, Joe-Joe nudged his head at a Foot Locker bag lying inside the trunk.

Excitedly reaching into the bag, Quran pulled out a shoebox and opened it to reveal a pair of the latest Le'Bron's. And they just happened to match his school's colors, which meant he could wear them for his upcoming game.

"Good-looking, dad!" he exclaimed, giving Joe-Joe a bear hug. "I love you more than anything."

As Joe-Joe climbed back inside the car and drove off, he was stung by a feeling of guilt. Because regardless of how he looked at it, he knew his lifestyle made it impossible for him to reciprocate his son's love.

Chapter 21

"Ayy, blood in my eyes/I'm goin' blind, oh/Stuck in these streets, feel like my life froze/I been runnin' these streets, got me dehydrated/I been livin' so crazy, feel like I'm dyin' baby . . ."
—Testimony

As Kodak Black bared his troubled soul on the track, Smoke was in his Bentley dangerously doing a buck-ten in the rain. On I-75 with the windshield wipers whipping back and forth, he held the wheel in one and a bottle of 1738 in the other. Thinking about the complexities of life, a fresh set of tears slid down his cheeks.

Since adolescence, Smoke's dream was to become a famous rapper with a wall full of platinum plaques. While enjoying the fortune and fame, he would support his loved ones, deliver a message on every album, and uplift his entire community. And his partner—Pistol—would be standing alongside him through it all. But the years passed and plans changed. A change that could be associated with one word: Loyalty.

His loyalty was the reason behind Pistol's death. His loyalty was the reason behind the three-year prison sentence that stalled his rap career. And his loyalty was the reason he was currently committed to the streets instead of music.

How long can this life last? He found himself thinking after Boss barely survived his encounter with death. *How many funerals will I attend . . . before somebody attending mine?*

The Wolf Pack were involved in enough criminal activities to have them in neighboring cells on death row. They were the constant target of jack boys. And they each slept with one eye open at night, wondering if their front door was moments away from being blitzed by federal agents. As Smoke considered all this, he was beginning to question if the foreign cars, fashion, and flawless stones were worth the many risks involved.

After all, how many street legends were in captivity with nothing left but memories that faded each passing year? And Smoke was certain that if you were to ask those men whether their present situation was worth the glory and gratification they received during their reign on the streets, majority would answer, "No." So who was he to think his outcome would be any different.

Bound by loyalty, the faithful soldier felt trapped in a war where medals were not awarded, and dungeons or death were the only means of escape.

***

Four days later . . .

Still recovering from his gunshot wounds, Boss summoned the immediate members of the Wolf Pack to a sit-down, which was currently being held at D-Wub's house out in Indian Hills. A neighborhood consisting of lawyers, doctors, and professional athletes, the drug lord had paid a half-million for the 4,000 square feet of property.

As the four men sat on the east balcony, which overlooked a lush landscaping and pebble-tech pool, Boss got straight to the matter at hand.

"I want out."

Amid expressions of shock, he continued, "I don't regret none of our time spent together, but I'm just ready to live life without having to constantly look over my shoulders or in my rearview."

In a Louie robe and matching slippers, D-Wub repeated, "You want out?"

Boss gave an affirmative nod. "Yeah, kid, I want out."

D-Wub glanced at Joe-Joe, who subtly shook his head; meaning he had no prior knowledge of this.

Scooting his chair back, D-Wub got up and produced a pocket-rocket from thin air. "Strip down to yo' draws, Blood," he told Boss.

"It ain't gon' happen," he calmly replied. "So you might as well shoot."

D-Wub cocked the hammer back. "Joe-Joe, I met this nigga through you," he spoke without taking his eyes off Boss. "So I'ma give you one chance to spare him."

"He ain't gotta spare me from *shit*," Boss said, as he stood up. "So if you gon' bust, then bust, nigga."

Joe-Joe stood up to intervene.

"Blood, you fooling right now," he scolded D-Wub. "This Boss we talking about. So put that gun up, my nigga."

After D-Wub lowered the gun, Joe-Joe convinced both men to take a seat, then asked Boss to explain his reason for wanting an early discharge. As a soldier who had proven himself on a number of occasions, he deserved to be heard.

Boss admitted that he being shot and nearly paralyzed was what initiated the change in his way of thinking. "Besides street shit, I realized that I don't even know what I'm good at. Like, what's my God-given talent. 'Cause ain't no way my purpose in life is just to kill shit, fuck hoes, and sell dope. So is something wrong with me wanting to find out who I am before it's too late?"

This being the most Boss had ever spoken at one time, he turned to stare Joe-Joe directly in his eyes and continued, "We got enough money to leave the game *right now*. So what the fuck is we waiting on . . . a federal indictment? You know I'll rot in that cell before I turn rat, my nigga. And I'm just trying to prevent that from happening."

Smoke felt him to the fullest, but it was not his place to speak up.

After gathering his thoughts, Joe-Joe reasoned with D-Wub, "He done gave us five years of uncontested loyalty, 'Wub. So what more can we ask for? If the man want out, then let him out."

Eyeing Boss with a scornful expression, D-Wub said, "When you return that chain I just copped you, make sho' it's a quarter-million with it."

"Gladly," he replied, with the same unblinking stare as D-Wub's.

While Joe-Joe was walking Boss outside to his car, Boss quietly informed him, "That nigga a dead man, Joe. He should've never pulled a gun out on me and not used it."

"I ain't justifying his actions, my nigga, but put yourself in his shoes. 'Cause you came out of nowhere with this shit. I love you like a brother, so it's only right that I keep it hundred with you.

And you was wrong, Boss. You should've come to me first, then we could've took it from there."

Reaching Boss's car, Joe-Joe continued, "Let that shit go for right now, bro. I'ma see where this nigga head at, and if I don't think he respect my wishes, then I'll give you a fair warning."

After the two friends shook-up and bear-hugged, Boss slid down inside his Nissan GTR and sped off without once looking back.

As Joe-Joe stood there watching the car until it disappeared out of sight, he had no idea he was only weeks away from wishing he had joined Boss in his timely departure.

Chapter 22

Lucasville

It was a little after midnight and J-Bo was buried beneath the covers quietly conversing with Heaven on his Galaxy. True to her word, she had brought Booka back two weeks later; during which time she and J-Bo embraced their undeniable chemistry. An angel in disguise, Heaven was resurrecting emotions he had deadened after the loss of Olivia.

On this particular night, Heaven was addressing what most men in prison feared the most—abandonment. "I'm fully aware of your situation, Javonte, and I know you can't help but entertain the idea that one day I'll just up and vanish. So as a result, you hold back from me, emotionally. But as I'm beginning to learn how good a person you really are, I could *never* leave you for dead in there. Even if I was to get married and have ten kids, I'll always be someone you can call on."

Despite J-Bo knowing the dangers of becoming emotionally attached to a female, especially while incarcerated, he believed she was being sincere. And besides, his primary concern was not with her sex life, but with her promise to keep Booka a part of his world.

As they continued to speak on a variety of subjects, Heaven casually slid in a question she had been wanting to ask for several days. "You've spoken so highly of your friendship with Juan-Juan, but why don't you ever talk about your mother?" Other than the fact that she died when he was young, he had never revealed anything else.

The line was silent for a minute before he finally admitted, "Because I don't have any good memories of her."

***

J-Bo's mind drifted towards a flashback . . .

Bang! Bang! Bang! Bang! Bang!

As her headboard repeatedly banged into the wall, nine-year-old Javonte covered his ears in an attempt to block out the loud and obscene noises coming from his mother's bedroom. She and her latest lover, Luther, were engaged in what was becoming a nightly routine.

Having dozed off, Javonte woke up in the middle of the night—to a now quiet house—and went upstairs to use the bathroom. When he finished peeing and turned to leave, he froze at the sight of Luther standing in the doorway.

Wearing only a pair of boxers and a perverted expression, Luther glanced over his shoulder before stepping inside the bathroom. "You a handsome lil' nigga, you know that?" he said while pulling the door closed.

His heart pounding in fear, Javonte took several steps back.

"You ain't gotta be scared, lil' man," Luther assured him, as he took several steps forward. "I know you think I be hurting yo' momma, on account of all the screaming she be doing. But I actually be making her feel good. If you'd just trust me, I could give you that same feeling."

When Javonte didn't respond, Luther took his silence as a sign of consent and reached toward him. Already knowing this moment would one day arrive, Javonte pulled a paring knife from the waistband of his pajamas and swung it with all his might.

Not long after his mother, Simone, and Luther began dating, Javonte noticed the looks Luther would slip him behind his mother's back. When he expressed his concerns to her, she angrily accused him of being delusional and threatened to beat him if he ever mentioned it again. Knowing he would have to protect himself, he started keeping the knife on him as if it was an asthma inhaler.

Luther backhanded Javonte into the tub before he looked down and saw blood squirting from his wrist. "This nigga done cut me," he mumbled in disbelief, then dizzily staggered against the sink and reached for a towel.

As Javonte was now crouched in the corner like a feral cat, Simone blew off into the bathroom in an untied robe and lit cigarette. "What the fuck going on in here?"

"That bastard over there cut me for no reason!" Luther lied, as he held a blood-soaked towel around his wrist. "Now call a muthafucking ambulance."

After Luther was rushed to the hospital, Simone asked Javonte what happened. "And you better not lie, either."

Needless to say, she not only refused to accept his version of events, but she also beat him with an extension cord for allegedly trying to sabotage her relationship with whom she claimed was a decent man.

While Javonte could forgive Simone for her addiction to men—which was the cause of him being neglected over the years—he would never recover from her decision to believe another man over him. So, from that day forward, he loved her as a mother, but disliked her as a person.

"I wish my real daddy would come get me," young Javonte would think to himself every night before falling asleep, the paring knife protectively placed beneath his pillow.

***

Like clockwork, J-Bo and Heaven wrapped up their conversation fifteen minutes prior to the first shift C.O.'s arrival on duty.

"A'ight, pretty, stay safe out there, and I'll try to call tonight."

"I'll be looking forward to it," Heaven said before yawning into the phone. "But if not, don't worry about it. Me and Booka will just see you Saturday."

After stashing the phone back in its hiding spot, J-Bo grabbed his music and began his morning ritual of 500 push-ups. With Booka and Heaven being a source of energy, he easily completed his exercise while vibing to Meek Mill.

"All the youngins in my hood popping percs now/Getting' high to get by, it's gettin' worse now/you gotta tell 'em put them guns and them percs down/Them new jails got ten yards in 'em and that's your first down . . ."

Chapter 23

After visiting Kiona's parents, she and Fat-Cat chartered a G6 and invited four of their friends on a spare-no-expense-trip to Vegas, where Gervonta 'Tank' Davis was scheduled to fight. This being Fat-Cat's favorite boxer, he purchased six tickets to the championship bout.

Fat-Cat brought Shooter and Blueface, while Kiona invited Samaria and Tab'—two women she befriended shortly after moving to Atlanta. Having developed a sisterly bond with the women over the years, they were both named god-mothers to her unborn child.

During their flight to Vegas, Fat-Cat popped a bottle of Champagne and everyone, besides Kiona, toasted to them having a healthy baby.

"And not that I'd be disappointed either way," Fat-Cat grinned after taking a generous sip, "But I've been secretly praying for a boy."

When the G6 landed in Vegas, two Presidential Sprinters were awaiting them, compliments of the Aria Sky Suites. Within the van's spacious interior was a bathroom, Apple TV, with Internet, refrigerator, and a microwave that sat beside a small refrigerator.

"Girl, this thing nicer than a lot of the houses I've lived in," Tab' joked, as she settled in the swivel seat and placed her feet in its power footrests.

The owner of a profitable boutique in east Atlanta, Tab' was an attractive twenty-year-old with no kids and a healthy appetite for success. While she was not opposed to meeting Mr. Right, she preferred to remain single until finding a man who could meet her simplistic standards.

Arriving at the Aria, they were welcomed by curbside concierges before being escorted inside to a private check-in lounge.

Dubbed 'The Hub of the new Vegas', Aria Sky Suites was a casino-cum-resort that was rated among the most luxurious hotels in the world. They had suites and villas stretching up to 6,000 sq. feet, with their surroundings being one of the most panoramic views of the city. At five-figures a night, it was a truly remarkable experience for those who could afford the finer things in life.

Once the women were inside their Villa, Samaria twirled in awe as she took in the expansive floor plan and state-of-the-art appliances.

"How did I get from the projects to this?" she asked no one in particular.

Born and bred in low income housing, the mother of one was the epitome of an ambitious woman who was determined to escape poverty. Using part-time stripping as a means to pay her way through college, Samaria received a degree in business and was now the proud owner of a hair-and-nail salon.

After blowing a check on their evening apparel, they went to have dinner before going over to the MGM. Known for its culinary experience, The Aria had an award-winning menu that included the table-side carving of Smoked Wagyu Brisket, prime Porterhouses, and Dover Piccata.

Digesting dishes they'd never heard of, they then went back to the Villas to prepare for the main event. This was Fat-Cat's first appearance at the MGM, and he intended to make a lasting impression on those in attendance.

***

Atlanta . . .

In a late model Impala, Malikah pulled into the driveway of her house as the sun was beginning to set. Having found a warehouse job several weeks ago, she had picked Booka up from daycare and desperately wanted to relax her tired feet.

Once inside the house, she fed and bathed Booka, then sat him in front of the Lion King before going to take a bath of her own. As she was on the verge of placing a foot inside the tub, she heard someone knocking at the front door.

I told this girl I was cool, Malikah said to herself while reaching for her robe.

Knock! Knock! Knock!

"I'm coming!" she yelled in irritation as she marched to the front door. Then, without thinking, she deactivated the alarm and snatched the door open.

"Can I help you?" Malikah asked, as she stared at the vaguely familiar face of a female.

Before the younger woman could respond, a hooded figure came from beside her and barged into the house.

Malikah couldn't believe her eyes as she was suddenly face-to-face with her ex-boyfriend, Deon. *How the fuck this nigga find me*? she wondered to herself, as she fearfully watched him close the door. *He must have given that bitch some money to make her knock on my door by way of distracting me so he could pull a stunt on me to get in my house.*

Since the morning of Malikah's disappearance, Deon and two of his men had been combing the streets of Atlanta. Assuming she'd eventually return to stripping, they would pop up in various clubs throughout the week. And just when he was beginning to think she might've left the city, Deon received a call from a female cousin who had recently moved in Malikah's neighborhood. "Her hair an' shit different, but it's definitely her, 'cuz."

True enough, it was a healthy-looking Malikah who Deon saw exit the car that evening as he sat parked across the street from her house.

"You looking real good, shawty," Deon lustfully commented, as he eyed Malikah's thickness through her sheer robe.

Cursing herself for not checking the peephole, she crossed her arms over her hardened nipples. "What do you want, Deon?"

With a playful smile, he replied, "Damn, that's how you greet a nigga after five months?"

When he reached out to untie her robe, she slapped his hand away. "Deon, stop, okay. I've moved on, and I just wish you would do the same."

He grabbed her by the throat and slammed her into the wall.

"Bitch, you can't tell me when to move on!" he spat, as he stuck his hand between her thighs. "I *own* you."

***

Struggling to breathe, Malikah was clawing at Deon's wrist when Booka came into the room.

"Get off my momma!" he yelled, as he ran down on Deon and started swinging.

Deon mugged him to the floor. "Watch out, lil' nigga."

Malikah went crazy.

As Deon was trying to subdue her, he hollered out in pain when Booka dug his teeth into the back of his leg. When he reached back to fight Booka off, this allowed Malikah to get loose and race into the living room, where she reached inside her purse and withdrew a .25 Terry Jones had given her for protection.

Punching Booka in the back of his head, Deon slung him across the room before going after Malikah. He froze in his tracks when she spun around with the semi-auto in shaky hands.

"Get the *fuck* out my house," she hissed in a venomous tone. "Or I swear to God I'ma blow yo' head off, nigga."

The look in her eyes enabled Deon to sense that she would squeeze if he took a step closer. So instead, he reached inside his hoodie and grabbed a small baggie. "You use to suck my dick for hours to get this shit. Remember that time—"

"You got five seconds before I pull this trigger," Malikah warned. "And I'm too close to miss."

Nodding, Deon smirked, "A'ight, shawty, you got it," then tossed the bag by her feet before turning to leave.

After locking the door behind him and setting the alarm, Malikah tucked the gun in the small of her back, then ran over to Booka and pulled him into her arms. "You a brave little man, you know that?" She lovingly crooned in his ear. "And momma love you to death."

As Malikah continued to whisper consoling words into her son's ear, her eyes were magnetically drawn to the bag of heroin lying only several feet away.

***

Back in Vegas . . .

With over 14,000 in attendance, the MGM Grand was packed for the Gervonta Davis fight. According to Money Mayweather, Gervonta was the next biggest thing in boxing.

Deliberately late, Fat-Cat and his entourage were led to their ring-side section seconds after the bell rung for the first round. While the ladies were expensively dolled-up and the gents' drip-game drew numberless nods of approval, Fat-Cat's appearance clearly indicated he was the head honcho.

In a throw-back Adidas tracksuit and low top Shell Toes, his jacket was left unzipped to showcase an array of diamond chokers and massive medallions that twinkled like mini stars. But there was one that stood out the most. Flooded with VVS's, it was a customized face of Jinx, with the letters 'MBK' attached to it in sapphire-blue diamonds.

With his chains alone exceeding a half-million, there was enough weight around Fat-Cat's neck to anchor a small boat.

Taking a seat beside Kiona, he draped an arm around her neck, displaying a bust down Rollie and ice-cube-size rings on all four fingers.

When Gervonta's hand was lifted in victory after a sixth round stoppage, Fat-Cat went live on Instagram. "I'm ringside at the MGM. The young bull Gervonta just retained his title in an *effortless* manner. Buddy survived the struggle, and you know we support our local troops."

On cue, Shooter and Blueface rose up and removed slabs of shekels from Fendi fanny packs. With Fat-Cat capturing the sensational scene on his three-camera iPhone, the two terrorists showered the crowd with $100,000.

As Fat-Cat was leaving, he happened to glance to his left and locked eyes with a famous rapper. Also draped in jewels, he slid Fat-Cat a slight nod, to which he respectfully returned the gesture.

You know you good when niggas like that acknowledging you, Fat-Cat smiled to himself as they left the arena.

Going to the Aria's high-limit casino, they gambled big while popping cork after cork.

Around two in the morning, Shooter pulled Fat-Cat aside. "Cuz, I met a nigga who work here that say for the right price, he can arrange an unforgettable night with some unforgettable hoes."

Normally, Fat-Cat would've readily agreed to what Shooter was suggesting, but he glanced over at his wife and realized something that made him decline the invitation.

Since day one, Kiona had been carrying herself like a woman worthy of being a wife. And more importantly, she would soon become the mother to his firstborn. As a woman who had not once violated his trust, it was clearly time to man-up and treat her accordingly as the queen she had proven herself to be.

So while Shooter and Blueface were in private rooms with women who spoke no English, Fat-Cat was in his Villa making love to his wife.

On Sunday morning the G6 flew them to the Windy City.

Piling inside a stretch Navigator at the airport, they were driven to the Bear's stadium, where they stood on the sidelines and cheered for Baby-Herc' as he led his team to a victory over the L.A. Rams.

Baby-Herc' was at a loss for words when Fat-Cat informed him of Kiona's pregnancy and the fact that he'd been chosen as the baby's godfather.

"You serious, Cuz?" he asked in disbelief, his eyes filling with tears of joy.

Fat-Cat smiled, "Is the sky blue, lil' nigga?"

While Fat-Cat entrusted Shooter and Blueface with the handling of his criminal enterprise, he knew that in the event of his demise Baby-Herc' would be a better father-figure, for he would ensure that his child chose a safer path in life.

After spending the day with Baby-Herc', Fat-Cat and the others tiredly climbed back on the jet and flew home, where an awaiting situation would soon have Fat-Cat back on another flight.

Chapter 24

Atlanta

When Terry Jones pulled up to Malikah's house and saw her car in the driveway, he instantly knew something was wrong. Because not only was her phone going straight to voicemail, but her supervisor had called to tell him that she hadn't been to work in two days. So, before exiting his Mark LT, Terry decocked an unregistered Ruger and tucked it in the small of his back.

After a sharp and unanswered knock at the front door, he let himself in and withdrew the semi while reaching up to deactivate the alarm. After checking the dining room and kitchen, he cautiously made his way upstairs.

On Malikah's bed lay a cellphone, which had a number of missed calls and texts. Her room and Booka's were empty.

He next approached the bathroom and saw that its door was partially opened. Taking a deep breath, he gripped the gun in both hands and nudged the door with the toe of his shoe.

Awkwardly bent against the bottom of the toilet, Malikah was lying on the floor with a purplish skin tone and lifeless eyes. A thin belt was still tightly fastened around her arm, the needle not far away. But what touched Terry the most was the image of a sleeping Booka cuddled up with his mother.

Booka had awakened in the middle of the night and found her laid out on the linoleum floor. Assuming she'd fallen asleep, he reached down to shake her arm. "Moma, wake up." When she didn't respond after several minutes, he lay down beside her and protectively placed his arms over her dead body.

Terry stuck the gun back in his pants before bending down to wake Booka. "Come on, lil' man, we gotta go."

Booka pushed his hand away and turned to Malikah. "Moma, wake up," he said in a pleading tone as he shook her arm.

Not knowing how to explain to a five-year-old that his mother was dead, Terry just scooped him up and left the bathroom.

"Let me go!" Booka cried, as he fought with a child's strength.

Carrying him from the house as he continued to kick and scream, Terry got inside the truck and held him tightly until he finally cried himself to sleep.

Then, gently laying him in the backseat, he brought the engine to life and drove off; the wheels in his mind also beginning to turn.

Regina and Heaven were already standing outside when Terry pulled into the driveway. While giving them a brief rundown, Heaven picked Booka up and carried him into the house. Known to him as auntie Heav', the two had grown close during their trips to visit J-Bo.

Inside the house, Terry went behind the bar and fixed himself and Regina a cocktail heavily laced with Johnny Walker.

"So what are we going to do, baby?" she inquired, accepting the glass.

His legs crossed as he thoughtfully twirled the glass of scotch, Terry answered, "Prevent that little boy from becoming a ward of the state."

Heaven was in her room stripping Booka down to his underwear as he lay asleep in her bed. She removed his jeans and noticed something in his back pocket. It was the picture of Juan-Juan that J-Bo had given him on their first visit. It brought tears to her eyes to know that Booka had been keeping his father's picture with him as if it was a beloved teddy bear.

Chapter 25

For informational purposes, Terry Jones had pocketed Malikah's phone. While several of the missed calls were from him, majority were from a number listed under BFF.

Calling the number, which belonged to a female, he stated that he was Malikah's landlord and was wondering if she had recently seen her. The female on the other end replied that she hadn't, but would give her a call. Then, as if she could sense something, she asked if everything was alright.

"You can talk to me," she quickly added. When she revealed she was the driver of the turquoise-colored car that had dropped Malikah off the day she signed the lease, Terry suggested they meet in person. He already knew through Malikah that this was one of her best friends.

An hour later, Terry Jones turned into Phipps Plaza and parked beside the turquoise BMW M5.

Standing outside in front of a boutique called 'First Class' was Kiona, who was Malikah's best friend.

Kiona and Malikah had become close several years ago. The two met when Malikah came into Kiona's newly opened boutique and spent $3,000. After learning that Malikah was a dancer at the Onyx, Kiona returned the supportive gesture by showing up at the club one night and drowning Malikah in a torrent of twenties.

Being two go-getters who shared similar core values, they developed a friendship that eventually evolved into something sisterly. In fact, it was Kiona Malikah had called on when she decided to leave Deon.

Kiona led Terry Jones inside her store, where half a dozen women were busily shopping.

"Danielle, I'll be in back if you need me," Kiona told an employee behind the register as she and Terry marched past.

When she opened the door of a small office, Fat-Cat was settled behind a desk in a business suit and tinted Carti's. He got up as they entered the room and came to stand beside his wife.

"Terry, this is my husband, Chris."

As they exchanged a firm handshake, Chris said, “Call me Fat-Cat.”

With there being no pleasant way to deliver bad news, Terry just came right out and informed them of Malikah’s death and the manner in which she had died.

Instantly stricken with grief, Kiona couldn’t believe her girl had relapsed. She had seen no warning signs, and Malikah appeared to have been doing so well.

“Oh my god, where’s Booka?” Kiona suddenly blurted out.

“I have him and he’s fine, Terry assured her. “I’m sure Malikah told you about him going to visit his uncle. And since they’ve developed a bond, I think it’s best that a visit be arranged as soon as possible. It’ll help him.”

Already knowing he was referring to J-Bo, Fat-Cat asked about his well-being.

“Considering his situation, he’s holding up pretty well.”

Fat-Cat reached in his pocket and withdrew a roll of hundreds. Without even counting it, he held it out to Terry. “Tell him I said whenever.”

After ensuring he would deliver the message and money, Terry asked Kiona if he could have a word with her husband.

Kiona looked at Fat-Cat, who gave her a subtle nod.

Once they were alone, Terry began, “I had cameras installed on the property I rented Malikah and I’d like for you to see it.”

Inserting the disk into a laptop, Fat-Cat watched the footage and confirmed that the man rushing into the house was Malikah’s ex, Deon.

Terry then removed a small baggie from his pocket and laid it on the table. It was the same bag of heroin Deon had given her.

“I had a friend of mine test this, and he says there’s enough Fentanyl in it to kill a large animal.”

While Malikah’s death appeared to have been an overdose, she had actually been murdered. Praying that she fell weak, Deon had intentionally laced the heroin with a deadly amount of the pharmaceutical opioid.

After nearly an hour of speaking in hushed tones, Terry Jones and Fat-Cat shook hands and agreed to link up again soon.

On his way out the store, Terry stopped to give Kiona his condolences.

"I know Malikah was your friend, and I'm sorry for your loss."

Kiona nodded, inwardly wishing she had been more persistent when Malikah denied the invite to Vegas. *She'd still be alive if I had convinced her to come*, she regretfully thought to herself.

As Fat-Cat accompanied Terry outside to his car, he assured him he would speak to his wife about there being no funeral for Malikah. "That lil' dude can't grow up like we did," he said in reference to Booka.

Opening the door to his Lincoln truck, Terry stuck one foot inside and solemnly swore, "I'd stand in front of a firing squad before I let that happen."

Terry Jones had never called 9-1-1 in regards to Malikah's death. Because to report it would put Booka at risk of becoming state property. So instead, he got rid of her body, car, and everything else inside the house that was associated with her.

He had made Juan-Juan a promise, and only death could prevent him from upholding it.

Chapter 26

Going ninety mph up I-75, D-Wub and September were half naked in the backseat of a chauffeured Navigator - Viceroy Edition. With the partition up and September screaming like a banshee, D-Wub had her going crazy.

"Ooh *fuck*, baby!" she shamelessly cried out, as her knees were beside her ears. "You killing this pussy!"

Trailing behind the armored SUV was Joe-Joe, Smoke, and Lil' Perry. In a Sierra Denali on 28's, the monster truck was pulling an enclosed trailer that had 'The Hulk' inside.

An hour later the two-car convoy got off on exit 71 and headed to National Trails, a popular drag strip in Columbus, Ohio. It was Test & Tune Thursday and the track would be packed with cheering spectators and gambling participants.

Upon their arrival, September camouflaged herself in a blonde wig and oversized Gucci shades. Despite the fact that they were out of town, this was a precaution she took whenever making public appearances with D-Wub.

In designer tags fresh off the racks and enough jewelry to open up their own Zales, the Wolf Pack made their way toward the quarter mile track.

"I don't think it's a nigga out here faster than me!" boasted a chubby man named Cheese, who was already on the track. He had the crowd's attention as he and his four-man entourage stood next to a Porsche 911 GT3.

"I'ma say it like this," he loudly continued, "I'm willing to give any man brave enough to race me a three-car head start." He then opened his arms in invitation and looked around. "Any volunteers?"

When it was clear no one was biting, D-Wub stepped from among the crowd. "I'll race you, but I don't need no head start."

While it was obvious D-Wub had money like the U.S. Treasury, Cheese was a brick-boy himself and refused to be intimidated. But before placing a wager, he curiously wanted to know who D-Wub was.

"Where you from, homie?" he questioned in a mild tone.

"That's irrelevant, Blood," D-Wub curtly answered. "Now is you trying race that lil' piece of shit or what."

"Piece of shit?" Cheese repeated. "Nigga, you looking at a two-hundred-thousand-dollar car. Fuck you talking 'bout!"

When he saw how attentive the crowd was, Cheese jumped out there.

"Matter fact," he said, as he reached inside the Porshe and grabbed a small Louie bag. "I gotta a hundred thousand dollars against *whatever* you bring to the line."

Without turning, D-Wub held up his hand and September appeared at his side with four stacks of money.

As D-Wub palmed the money, he said, "On top of this, let's bet them pink slips, too."

A suspenseful silence overcame the crowd as they awaited Cheese's response.

With his heartbeat threatening to burst from inside his chest, he glanced at his crew, who gave him a subtle head-shake. Because not only was D-Wub overly confident, but they didn't even know what he was bringing to the line.

Unable to stifle his pride, Cheese ignored his men and took the bet. He would rather lose his car and money than to simply stand down. *Chances make champions*, he told himself as D-Wub went to go get The Hulk.

With the trailer positioned to where the crowd couldn't see inside, they watched in wonder as D-Wub entered a side door, while Joe-Joe hit a button that made the back end lower into a ramp.

When D-Wub climbed behind the wheel and brought the beast to life, instead of immediately backing it out, he revved its powerful engine, causing the whole trailer to start rocking.

"What the fuck he got in there!?" one man said, as it seemed like the trailer was on the verge of tipping over.

The crowd was in awe when D-Wub backed the car out with its top slowly retracting. Candy-apple green over white guts, it was a '71 Dodge Challenger on forged Mickey Thompson's. With The Hulk's heart being a 440 Hemi and his lungs a 727 trans., the masculine machine was gorgeous enough to grace the cover of a duPont Registry.

Cheese was sweating bullets by the time they pulled up to the line. And as he dreadfully listened to the Hemi heavily breathing beneath the cowl hood, he knew there was no margin for error. Had they been going the distance, it would've been like taking candy from a baby. But this was just a quarter-mile, which meant anything could happen.

His right hand gripping the detachable wheel, D-Wub locked the front brakes and stood on the gas. The back tires screaming as the car slightly fishtailed in place, this was simply to warm the Mickey's up for better traction when he took off. With over eighty grand invested under the hood, this was a true ten-second car.

Having only one loss under his belt, which was when he initially started racing, D-Wub's belief was that muscle cars beat imported vehicles in most quater-mile races. Especially when you handpicked opponents whose arrogance overshadowed their experience. He had been racing in cities all over the Midwest, and there was a Cheese in each one.

***

When the light turned green, D-Wub's reaction time allowed him to instantly hit his break release.

Vroooooooooooooooooooooom!

Exhaling a monstrous roar as it rocketed forward, The Hulk's front end rose off the ground for the first ten feet.

As they were gaining momentum down the track, Cheese was a car length ahead when fear made him commit a costly mistake. He over-revved the engine while shifting into second and missed his gear.

Inside The Hulk, D-Wub was smiling as the 727 went into third.

With the back-end of the Challenger squatted low to the ground, Cheese could only helplessly watch as it barreled toward the finish line.

"Fuck!" he hollered out, banging his fist into the steering wheel.

As they turned around and headed back to the starting line, Cheese reached under his seat and grabbed a 17-round Berretta. "This nigga got me fucked up," he mumbled to himself.

The crowd was excitedly gathered on the track as D-Wub and Cheese exited their cars.

"You can have the money," Cheese said, as his hand lingered near his waist. "But I'm keeping my whip."

D-Wub looked at Joe-Joe and smiled, "This nigga fooling, ain't he?"

"Naw, nigga, *you* fooling," Cheese cut in. "Now get the fuck on before I change my mind about you keeping the money."

Telling Lil' Perry to grab The Hulk, D-Wub was marching back to the Navigator when he recited the Porsche's plate number to September.

"Get me his address."

"Baby, I don't think—"

"I ain't ask you what you think. A nigga ain't never chalked me for *nothing* and lived. Now get me his muthafucking address!"

D-Wub's plan was for everybody to go back to Cincinnati, while him and Lil' Perry went on a quick field trip.

As D-Wub was in the passenger seat of The Hulk removing his jewelry, he received a jail call from Ghost. *Not right now, homie*, he said to himself, as he hit the decline icon.

September got out the truck and walked over to him with Cheese's address written on a napkin.

"Please be careful, De'," she said, as she passed it to him.

While D-Wub was someone she cherished and wanted to spend the rest of her life with, September was beginning to wonder if his barbaric ways made him incapable of reciprocating the same type of love.

Before driving off, D-Wub gave her his jewelry and point of view. "Ain't no need for worrying, 'cause this shit already written."

***

Lebanon Prison

After calling D-Wub's phone several times and getting no answer, Ghost slammed the receiver down and angrily went back to his cell.

"Blood, I need some space!" he barked at his cellie, who was on the top bunk watching TV.

Despite being in the middle of a good movie, his cellie kept his attitude in check as he jumped down and left the room.

Covering the window on his door with a strip of cardboard, Ghost grabbed two quarts of homemade wine out of his locker box and started chugging.

He was halfway through the second jug when he began to feel the effects of the potent juice and got emotional.

"That nigga 'Wub don't give a fuck about me," he vented to himself, using the back of his hand to wipe his mouth. "Like I ain't the reason he ain't in this bitch doing life."

Ghost had never thrown it in D-Wub's face, but it was his Glock .40 that was found the night they killed Jinx. And the medical report clearly stated that the victim had died from the initial gunshot wound to his heart, which had come from a .40 caliber handgun. So in all actuality, Ghost was doing a life sentence for a body that wasn't even his.

"All I asked him to do was hold me down," Ghost continued. "And that nigga put it on *blood* he had me!"

The loyal soldier wasn't blowing D-Wub's phone up looking for a handout. He just wanted to inform him that his mom was dying from breast cancer and didn't have much longer to live. All alone as she lay in a hospice bed, and he needed D-Wub to go see her before it was too late.

With regret nibbling away at his soul, Ghost wanted him to explain to her how much her son loved her and how remorseful he was for the heartache he caused her over the years. But with D-Wub not answering his phone in nearly a month, it seemed he might miss out on the closure he desperately needed.

"I literally gave my *life* for you, Blood," Ghost said, as a single tear slid down his cheek. "And you ain't even here for me when I need you the most."

***

Back in Columbus . . .

It was dark outside when Lil' Perry pulled up beside a Buick Grand National and let D-Wub out.

Adrenaline coursing through his veins, he used a Slim Jim to get inside the car and peeled the column in under two minutes. *Shit like riding a bike*, he smiled to himself as he pulled in behind Lil' Perry and followed him to the interstate.

Fifteen minutes later, they got off on an exit in Blacklick—a suburban section on the city's east side, and D-Wub had Lil' Perry wait in the darkened parking lot of a bar called McGoo's.

"I'll be right back," he told him before driving off.

D-Wub thanked the game god when he drove past Cheese's house and saw the Porsche sitting in the driveway.

Parking at the end of the block, he tucked a Glock .21 in his pants and soldiered back down the street.

Boldly walking up to the Porsche, D-Wub kicked it hard enough to set off the alarm, then crouched down onside of Cheese's house and waited.

***

It wasn't long before the porch light cut on and Cheese came flying out the house in his boxers, discreetly holding a handgun down at his side.

Silencing the alarm, he glanced up and down the street for any sign of movement, checked the Porsche for damages, then turned to go back inside and came face-to-face with the boogeyman.

Frozen in fear as a drop of piss trickled from his penis, Cheese couldn't believe his eyes.

Wearing a sinister smile as he held the Glock within inches of Cheese's face, D-Wub nodded in affirmation. "Yeah, nigga, it's me."

Cheese opened his mouth to plead and D-Wub squeezed.

Pow! Pow!

As he lifelessly fell onto the car and slowly slid down it, D-Wub was already marching back to the Grand National.

Instead of going back to the bar, D-Wub called Lil' Perry and said to meet him on the interstate. "I'ma be on side of the road with my hazards on."

When Lil' Perry pulled over on the interstate as if he was a concerned citizen, D-Wub hopped in the car and they merged back into traffic.

Meanwhile, the ambulance and CPD were arriving at the murder scene.

Unbeknown to D-Wub, Cheese's girl had witnessed the shooting from an upstairs window. Calling 9-1-1 as she ran outside, she saw blood pooling from the two holes in his face and hysterically began screaming for the dispatcher to send an ambulance.

In their police report, authorities would state that they found the deceased victim seated on the ground, clutching a gun in his left hand. With his face frozen into a fearful expression, his head was lying right beside the Porsche emblem on the front wheel of his car.

Pride.

That was reason for Cheese's death. He had been unaware of the wise saying: 'Pride goes before a fall.'

Chapter 27

Cincinnati

"Did you tell daddy about my recital this weekend?" a ten-year-old girl asked her mother, as they were leaving her evening dance class.

"I sure did," the mother answered with a smile. "And he said to tell you he wouldn't miss it for anything in the world."

"He did?"

While the girl's father provided her with every material thing she could possibly want, his commitment to the streets prevented her from often receiving what she craved the most—his presence.

As they climbed inside a Jeep and drove off, the woman told her daughter to check the center console. "I think your father left you something in there."

She screamed in excitement when she saw it was a new iPhone. "I gotta call daddy and—"

Crash!

The driver side of the Jeep was suddenly T-boned by a conversion van, which two masked men quickly hopped out of. Running to either side of the Jeep, they snatched open its doors, cut the seat belts, then threw the disoriented mother and daughter over their shoulders and raced back to the van.

Screeeeeeeeeeech! The tires of the van grated the tarred road harshly, as the kidnappers rounded a corner and sped off, leaving the Jeep in the intersection with both doors open.

Witnesses would say the incident took place in less than a minute.

***

Inside a hotel room, Hiram and three others were wiping down shell casings and cleaning guns. After burying six of his own, he had finally gotten the drop on D-Wub's whereabouts. A female spy had sent him a text saying the drug lord was currently at a high stakes gambling house in Lincoln Heights.

Hiram was strapping on a bulletproof vest when his phone started ringing. Assuming it was the female calling with more Intel, he grabbed the phone and slid his thumb to the right.

Instantly seized by a number of emotions—mainly fear—Hiram stared in shock at an image of his ten-year-old daughter. While tied to a chair with a blindfold over her eyes and duct tape covering her mouth, a masked man stood several few feet away, holding a menacing looking Pit Bull. To prove this was presently occurring, another phone showing the date and time was held in front of his daughter.

"You got thirty minutes to be at Oakley's on John and Popular," warned the voice of a masked man. "A minute late, and we gone let Damu go. And he ain't ate all day."

The kidnappers showed the face of his daughter one last time before disconnecting the call.

Flying into a fit of rage, Hiram threw his phone and grabbed an AK-47 by the barrel. His men stepped out of harm's way as he used the assault rifle like a baseball bat and destroyed the room.

Once Hiram got tired and there was nothing left to break, he turned to face his men with a deeply disturbed look.

"What's good, bro?" his right-hand, Benny, asked in genuine concern.

Now standing still as a statue, Hiram answered in defeat, "They got my daughter, Ben."

Hiram was clueless as to how D-Wub had found his daughter. Because not only were his own family members unaware of where she and the mother lived, but he had always been careful whenever he went to see them out in Batavia. Although it was too late, Hiram now realized the mistake he'd made in underestimating the thoroughness of his opponent.

Hiram popped a Perc' and washed it down with a swallow of Hennessey.

"Benny, you know where everything at," he said, while wedging his strap in the front his pants. "So if I don't make it back, I'ma need you to make sure everybody good."

Fueled off loyalty, Benny threw a hoodie on over his vest and snatched up a Draco. "I'm coming with you."

Hiram shook his head. "Nah, not this time, homie. I gotta do this alone."

"I know this ain't what you trying to hear, bro, but in a situation like this, you already know what the outcome is."

"Then so be it," Hiram replied with a shrug. "'Cause ain't way I could ever look myself in the mirror if I didn't show up for my lil' girl."

Hiram paused before leaving out the door, turned back to give his men a double salute, then courageously carried on.

"Man, that nigga fooling," a soldier named Hobo said after the door closed.

"Nah," Benny shook his head in disagreement. "That the realest nigga I ever met."

Chapter 28

Turning into the darkened scrap yard, Hiram slowly drove through it till he came upon a pair of headlights. He brought his car to a stop and threw it in park.

Appearing out of nowhere, two masked men with sawed-offs approached his car from either side and ordered him to step out.

Once out of the car, Hiram was frisked by one of the men and stripped of his phone and firearm.

In hooded sweat suits and construction boots, Shake-D and Tilla then emerged from the car ahead.

"I'm here," Hiram said, with his arms spread outward. "Now where my daughter at?"

Staring with hatred at the man responsible for taking the life of his baby brother, Shake-D answered Hiram with a leaping left hook that put him straight to sleep.

Shake-D had gone on a three-day killing spree after the death of his brother, Rum. And there was not a man, woman, or child he wouldn't murder in his pursuit of payback. But once again, it was Tilla who helped him see the error in his thinking.

"We killing off shit that don't mean nothing, and that's why he still hiding. But once we find his weakness, we won't have to keep looking for him . . . 'cause he gon' come to us."

True enough, after doing their homework and handing out hundred dollar bills as if they were fliers, they eventually learned the name of Hiram's baby's mother. They gave the name to D-Wub and the rest was history.

After hog-tying Hiram and throwing him into the trunk of a Caprice, Tilla and Shake-D got inside the car and pulled off. They were headed to a small town called Cleaves— which was on the border of Ohio and Indiana.

As Shake-D handled the wheel, Tilla called the kidnappers and spoke three words, "Let 'em go." Since Hiram had paid the ransom, there was no need in killing an innocent woman and her child.

Arriving in Cleaves, they followed the directions D-Wub had given them and were soon turning onto a dirt road. As if he could sense what was in store for him, Hiram began thrashing around in the trunk.

When they pulled the Caprice up to a large barn, a bear-size white man was standing outside shouldering a Remington shotgun.

As they emerged from the car, the hillbilly spat out a glob of tobacco juice and asked, "How many ya bring?"

"Just one," Tilla said, as he passed him an envelope containing ten thousand dollars.

"Well, grab him and let's go."

When they popped the trunk and grabbed Hiram, he did his best to show no sign of fear. During the ride, he had mentally prepared himself to withstand whatever manner of torture they used in trying to break him.

But his resolve instantly weakened when they entered the barn and he heard the loud, sickening sounds of grunts and squeals. *These niggas about to feed me to some fucking pigs*, he thought to himself in sheer terror. This was beyond anything he had imagined.

The hillbilly led them over to a small pit, where three 600-pound 'Russian Red' hogs were hungrily staring up at them. The most vicious hog known to mankind, they could consume a human body in less than twenty minutes.

"I ain't fed 'em in ten days, so you can just imagine how good and hungry they is." He then pointed to a sledge hammer lying nearby. "One of ya take that and crack his skull and pelvic bone, and we'll get this lil' party here started."

This being opposite of what Shake-D had in mind, he asked, "Why we gotta crack his skull and shit?"

"Cause those the only parts a hog can't get into their mouths."

Shake-D pulled out a small bankroll and offered it to the hillbilly. "This a extra five-grand if you let us throw him in there alive."

He grunted, spit out another glob of brown juice and said, "You'll definitely be making' my job harder, but hell, gone and throw him in there."

Wanting to hear Hiram scream, Shake-D snatched the tape off his mouth before he and Tilla picked him up,

"You niggas is bitches!" Hiram spat, as they carried toward the pit. "And that's why I killed yo' bitch-ass brother!"

Hiram was still slinging obscenities and spit when they dropped him down into the pit.

As the starving hogs immediately sunk their teeth into Hiram, he let out a piercing scream that was unlike anything Tilla had ever heard. When one of the hogs tore open his stomach and greedily began to chew his intestines, Tilla had to look away.

Tuned in to the gruesome ordeal as if it was an episode of the 'Wire', Shake-D wore a sinister smile as he watched the hogs eat Hiram alive.

Once the horrific display was finally over, Shake-D turned to the hillbilly and promised, "I'll definitely be seeing you again."

Chapter 29

With her hair wrapped in a bath towel, September was coming out the bathroom when she heard her dog, Pepper, downstairs going crazy.

"Pepper, get up here!" she yelled on her way into the bedroom. She didn't even have to look to know that he was in the front window barking at the dog next door as it came out for its morning defecation.

September was stuffing her ripe breasts inside a bra when Pepper came charging into the room.

"What's moma's boy doing, huh?" she said in a singsong tone, as she reached down to play with him. "You being a bully down there?"

Already running late, she played with him a minute longer and resumed getting dressed.

In a Simon Miller pantsuit and soft-soled flats, September locked the dog in the basement, then stopped in the kitchen to holster her service weapon. Looping her badge around her neck as she left out through the side door, she was now officially Detective September McGee.

Inside the garage, she hit the button to raise its door as she was climbing into her car. She cut on some Ella Mai, then turned in her seat to back out and saw six ski-masked SWAT members rushing in.

"Shut the car off!" the lead man ordered, as he stood outside her window with an MP5.

Killing the engine, it suddenly dawned on her what Pepper had been barking at.

Once out of the car and relieved of her weapon, she was handcuffed and placed in the backseat of a heavily tinted Yukon.

A SWAT member climbed behind the wheel of the SUV and pulled off his mask. It was her superior and lover, Detective Anthony Flowers.

"Tell me something," he said, turning in his seat to face her. "Did you honestly believe you could be involved with the biggest drug dealer in this city and I wouldn't eventually find out?"

Despite the fearful pounding of her heart, September returned his stare and calmly replied, "Baby, I don't know what you're talking about. This has to be a misunderstanding."

Scoffing at her response, he removed several photos from a manila envelope and held one up. "So I guess this isn't your house?" he said, holding up a photo that showed D-Wub leaving out through the backdoor.

"And I guess this is the twin sister you forgot to tell me about," he said, holding up another photo that clearly showed her and D-Wub exchanging a kiss outside the hotel in Kentucky.

As September blankly stared at the photos, she felt like she had suddenly been placed in the cockpit of a descending plane.

Detective Flowers had spotted them the day September ran out the hotel to give D-Wub his phone. She had been in such a rush that she forgot to disguise herself. And Flowers just happened to be leaving a fishing store across the street when he saw who appeared to be her frantically flagging down the Escalade.

When he curiously reached inside his car for a pair of binoculars, he disbelievingly watched as she handed the known drug lord something before embracing him in a kiss that clearly indicated they had history. Sizzling with anger behind the burn of her betrayal, he then began tracking her every move.

Knowing the game is designed for the 'house' to win, September had sensed that a losing hand was on the verge of being dealt to her and D-Wub. She tried to warn him it was time to cash-in, but because he had grown addicted to the euphoric feeling of winning, he insanely believed they were incapable of crapping out.

Dreadfully realizing where her loyalty was about to lead her, she could only imagine the treasonous charges which she was facing.

As if reading her mind, Detective Flowers informed her of her fate while placing the photos back inside the manila envelope.

"That license plate number you ran the other day belonged to a woman named Brandy Pines. And it turns out, her fiancé was murdered that night. So among your slew of charges, you're also looking at complicity to commit aggravated murder."

Eyeing her through the rearview mirror, Flowers said, "The blonde wig wasn't enough."

When September looked up, he smiled, "Yeah, I know all about the incident at the race track. So you'll be *lucky* if you escape the death penalty . . . Detective Traitor McGee."

Chapter 30

Twenty thousand feet above the earth, Fat-Cat was on a chartered flight to Jamaica to link up with Graveyard, whom he had remained in touch with after their initial encounter, several years ago. He couldn't save the world, but he also couldn't cross paths with a good man and overlook his struggle. So every Christmas he wired the Jamaican a generous present.

In a linen short set and several gold chains, Graveyard was already waiting at the airport when Fat-Cat's plane landed. While he didn't normally show emotion in public, the dread-head couldn't help but smile as he greeted the man responsible for remodeling his life.

"Rude bwoy!" he exclaimed, gripping Fat-Cat's hand in a firm shake.

They climbed inside a four-door Benz and sped down the rural roads of Kingston while exchanging light conversation. According to Graveyard, he was not only a club owner, but also the biggest weed distributor in his parts.

"So tell me, rude bwoy," he said, as he plucked a half-smoked stogie out the astray and sparked it. "Wiyah mek such long trip tuh Jamaica?"

Declining the stick of weed, Fat-Cat said he had a proposition that would make him the king of Kingston if he were to accept. Already knowing the island's value of an American dollar, he turned to look at Graveyard and added, "I'm talking 'bout a quarter-million in cash."

As the monster in him instantly awakened, Graveyard flicked the blunt out the window and replied in a deadly tone, "Gunz dem uh bust, rude bwoy."

Occasionally nodding, the Jamaican gangster was all ears as Fat-Cat began to explain what he needed done.

***

Mechanicsville, Georgia . . .

Deon was sloppy drunk as he and a voluptuous vixen staggered out of Young Dro's after-hour at three in the morning. His pockets $500 lighter, he had solicited her services for several hours at a nearby motel.

Helping her into the passenger seat of his Suburban, Deon squeezed one of her meaty thighs and slurred, "I'ma beat the lining out this pussy!"

"You better," she said, before licking his lips with her lizard-like tongue.

Anxiously closing her door, Deon was coming around the front of his truck when Shooter rose up from a crouched position, clutching a Glock 26.

"This for Malikah," he said before he put one in Deon's face, then stood over him and fired four more.

Pow! Pow! Pow! Pow!

As the female inside the truck hopped out and ran, Shooter took off in the opposite direction, jumped in a hotbox and hauled ass.

The killing had been at the request of Terry Jones. He'd made it clear to Fat-Cat that on the strength of Juan-Juan, he would pay whatever fee necessary to ensure that Deon's electricity was cut off.

Because he and Juan-Juan had crawled out the same mud, Fat-Cat told Terry he couldn't accept his money, but would make arrangements to have his wishes fulfilled in a timely fashion. "I'll put my right-hand-man on it," Fat-Cat had said.

Hunting Deon down with no accomplice, Shooter had put his head to bed in less than two weeks.

***

Six hours after arriving in Jamaica, Fat-Cat was back on the private jet. He had proposed his plan to Graveyard and the gangster had readily come aboard. It was now only a matter of time.

They were flying over the Atlantic. But all of a sudden, the plane was rocked by heavy turbulence, causing champagne to spill from Fat-Cat's glass. Before panic could fully settle in, an attendant came to calmly announce that they were on the verge of making an emergency landing.

Fat-Cat was far from being religious, but during their dangerous descent toward earth he was earnestly asking God to let him live long enough to witness the birth of his firstborn.

His prayer was answered when the pilot made a bumpy but successful landing on a runway in Florida. He apologized for the inconvenience and informed Fat-Cat they would be back in the air as soon as the weather permitted.

Grateful to be alive, Fat-Cat couldn't even complain as he went inside the crowded airport to find a place to sit. *A nigga might have to go to church when I get back to the crib*, he said to himself, as he dialed Kiona's number.

As he and his wife were face-timing, a female voice called his name.

"Fat-Cat?"

He looked up and couldn't believe his eyes. It was Neicy. Telling Kiona he'd call her back, he stood up to give Neicy a hug.

"Boy, what you doing way down here in Florida?" she asked, as they broke apart.

While explaining that he was coming from a business trip in Jamaica, he gave Neicy a once-over and couldn't deny that she was looking good. Her hair and make-up flawless, she had her curvaceous figure conservatively concealed beneath a pinstripe pantsuit and authentic Red Bottoms.

"So where you end up settling down at?" Fat-Cat inquired, as he recalled their last encounter outside her house.

***

Smiling proudly, Neicy told him that she had gone to New York and fulfilled her dream and Ciara's—opening up a daycare for disabled children. The business idea an instant success, she now owned several daycares through the state.

"But more importantly," she continued, while looking over at Savannah as she busily played a handheld video game, "I was able to save that little girl's life."

Upholding her promise to Ciara, Neicy had spared no expense when it came to taking care of Savannah. After locating a highly qualified specialist of her own, the nine-year-old's cancer was now in full remission.

As they continued to fill each other in on the last four years of their lives, Fat-Cat learned that Neicy had lost Suge's baby due to a miscarriage. While she was distraught over the death, she gained the strength to carry on by understanding that every occurrence in life had a valid reason behind it, even if she couldn't presently see it. *God don't make mistakes*, she would often remind herself.

Before parting ways, Neicy invited Fat-Cat over to meet Savannah. As he shook her small hand and took in the brightness of her smile, he was suddenly struck by a realization that hit him harder than the wisdom from Kiona's father.

Ciara would miss her daughter's every experience. And her absence in this beautiful child's life was no one's fault but her own. True enough, Savannah may have had Neicy, but she would forever yearn for the love and support from her biological mother; a familiar feeling Fat-Cat knew all too well. And if he was to prevent his own child from possibly wandering down that same painful path, then he had no choice but to make certain adjustments in his life, regardless of the cost.

I gotta be a better man than the father I never met, he would conclude to himself during his flight back to Atlanta.

Chapter 31

Cincinnati

Inside a packed U.C. arena, Joe-Joe, D-Wub and Smoke were sitting courtside at Quran's state championship game. His team was up two points with only a minute left and the scent of victory hung heavily in the air.

Playing aggressive defense as if it were his team losing, Quran managed to steal the ball and took off on a fast break. This being the moment he'd been praying and preparing for all season, he threw the ball high off the glass when he got near the free throw line.

With the crowd watching in awe as he rose up, he palmed the ball in midair, with one hand, and slammed it like LeBron James.

As the arena went into an uproar and his teammates excitedly rallied around him, Quran locked eyes with his father and saluted.

Joe-Joe felt an immense sense of pride while watching photographers snap dozens of pictures of his son holding up the championship trophy. The boy was definitely gifted, and Joe-Joe was doing everything possible to ensure he one day became an N.B.A. candidate.

The primary sponsor for his son's team, he had secretly secured him an invitation to an AAU summer tournament in North Carolina. He would surprise him with the news when they went out to eat after the game.

They were leaving the arena when Quran playfully bumped into D-Wub and asked him if he liked the dunk.

"Come on, Blood," he smiled, placing an arm around Quran's neck. "You already know that was the highlight of the game." He then slyly slid him a thousand dollars, which was something he did after each of his victories.

Pulling off in a powder blue Bentley truck, they went to Ruth Cris and went overboard on steaks and crab cakes.

Joe-Joe paused in the middle of eating and told Quran about the AAU invitation.

He stopped chewing and looked up in disbelief. "You serious?"

Joe-Joe removed the letter from his pocket and laid it on the table.

His mouth still full of food, Quran snatched it up, quickly read over it, then pumped his fist triumphantly. "Hell yeah!"

"Boy, chew ya food up," Joe-Joe laughed. "You spitting shit everywhere."

"Don't forget about me when you make it to the league," Smoke said jokingly. "Cause you know I'm yo' favorite uncle."

"Blood, you fooling!" D-Wub cut in, as he winked at Quran. "This lil' nigga know he's like the son I never had."

While they continued to joyfully converse and suck the food's flavors from their fingertips, Joe-Joe said he needed to stop by his house before dropping Quran off. He had one more surprise.

As they were leaving the restaurant, Quran told Joe-Joe he knew he had another surprise for him and begged for a hint.

Playing dumb, Joe-Joe replied, "I don't know what you talking about."

"Come on, dad, you know—"

"FBI! Get on the ground! Get on the ground!"

Appearing from everywhere in tactical clothing with laser-sighted submachine guns, nearly two dozen FBI agents surrounded them.

Out of concern for his son's safety, Joe-Joe instantly complied and yelled for Quran to follow suit. With police shootings being a worldwide epidemic, he knew they would use any excuse to open fire.

Lying down beside his son, Joe-Joe spent their final moments together urging him to stay on the right track. "Whatever you do, don't let nothing or nobody knock you off yo' pivot. Not even me."

"But what I'ma do without you, dad?" Quran tearfully asked. His dad was his best friend.

"You gon' man-the-fuck-up!" Joe-Joe hissed, as he was being placed in handcuffs. "You gon' stay in school and keep hooping. And in the end, I promise you it's gon' pay off."

As Joe-Joe was being led away, he looked back at Quran and mouthed the words, 'I love you'.

Blinking back tears, he nodded, "I love you too, dad."

Quran would later learn that the surprise was something he'd been wanting for years, the reuniting of his parents. After recently ironing out their differences, they decided it would be best if the next five years of his life was spent in a two-parent household.

So during the game—which he thought his mother had missed—she and a team of movers were transporting their belongings from Kentucky to Cincinnati. She was supposed to yell 'Surprise!' when they walked through the front door. But unfortunately, that occasion would now never occur.

Oddly, Smoke felt a sense of relief as he was being driven downtown. Tired of wondering when this inevitable day would arrive, he was just ready to face his fate and get it over with.

The agent transporting D-Wub glanced in his rearview and decided to disturb the drug lord's look of tranquility.

"You think you got it all figured out, huh, big man?"

When D-Wub didn't respond, he continued, "You're probably thinking, worst case scenario, you'll get ten and be out in six or seven with good behavior. But I got news for you. The only way you're getting ten is if you snitch on every crook you've ever met. Otherwise, you're looking at a life sentence. And the feds don't have a parole board."

Still staring out the tinted window, D-Wub didn't respond.

"Oh, and there's one other thing I forgot to mention. A friend of yours asked me to apologize on her behalf. She said hurting you was the only way to help herself."

D-Wub cut his eyes up front and the agent smirked. "Yeah, I thought that would get your attention. Trust me when I tell you . . . you're *cooked*, motherfucker."

Chapter 32

Atlanta

In a Prada peacoat and Saint Laurent boots, Fat-Cat was standing outside his barbershop when Shooter drove up in an Ocean-Blue Wraith.

Look at my lil' youngin', Fat-Cat smiled to himself while approaching the passenger side of the coupé.

Settling into the seashell-colored cabin, he extended his hand along with a compliment, then told Shooter to drive out to Mechanicsville.

As they were gliding through the city beneath a roof full of stars, Fat-Cat removed his Carti's and made a startling three-worded statement. "I'm done, Shooter."

A bust down Rollie glistening on his wrist as he handled the wheel, Shooter briefly took his eyes off the road to glance at Fat-Cat. "You done?"

He nodded. "Yeah, homie, I'm full. So I'm excusing myself from the table."

Turning to Shooter, Fat-Cat asked, "Care to join me?"

A slight grin appeared on Shooter's face before he answered, "Nah, Cuz, I'm still hungry."

That being the answer he expected, Fat-Cat replied, "Then I guess it's only right that you take yo' seat at the head of the table."

Shooter was instantly submerged into a sea of euphoria, as he suddenly understood he was on the verge of becoming his own boss. Despite loyally playing his position over the years, this was the moment he had been anxiously awaiting.

As he was expressing his gratitude and assuring Fat-Cat he was ready to fulfill the role, they arrived at a beige, three-story house.

"Come on, I wonna show you something," Fat-Cat said, exiting the car.

Inside the fully furnished house, Fat-Cat deactivated the alarm and led Shooter into a kitchen with ceramic tile flooring and state-of-the-art appliances. He went over to an LG refrigerator, pulled it away from the wall, then punched in a series of numbers on the refrigerators' front screen.

Exhaling a soft click, the back of the refrigerator came ajar. When Fat-Cat opened it all the way, Shooter stared in awe at the jars full of pills that were lined up on several rows of built-in shelves.

Fat-Cat then surprised him for a second time, by saying, "This all you, my nigga, free of charge. And when you done with these, the plug waiting on you with a fresh shipment."

Goosebumps broke out all over Shooter's arms. This was a graduation ceremony he would've never expected.

"Cuz, you can call on me as long as I got oxygen in my body," Shooter stated in his most sincere tone. "I don't give a fuck if it's a kidney transplant or the killing of a *Reverend Mother*. All you gotta do is let me know. And, on Geer Gang Crip, I got you."

As they were driving back to the city, Shooter lowered the music and asked out of curiosity, "Cuz, I respect yo' decision, but why the sudden change of heart?"

"I'm literally about to be a father, homie. So it ain't like I'm only living for myself no more, you feel me. I gotta be there for my seed. And raising a child is a serious responsibility, one that I refuse to forsake or take lightly. So regardless of how smooth I think I'm stepping, or how little I'm getting my hands dirty, being in the streets is a risk I just can't keep taking."

Fat-Cat paused for a moment, then continued. "I ain't gon' lie and say I ain't gon' miss the thrill of getting money. But at the end of the day, I had to make a choice. And I chose to put my seed before *anything* that could prevent me from physically being present in their life. 'Cause like a wise man recently told me, 'You can't be a good father from a graveyard or cemetery."

Before parting ways, Fat-Cat informed Shooter of D-Wub's situation, which he had heard about through word of mouth. "Look like buddy's reign done ran its course."

Despite the fact that D-Wub was a nemesis, he had been prepared to annihilate Fat-Cat found no joy in the man's current situation. But at the same time, he was grateful for his decision to switch lanes before being involved in a similar accident.

Chapter 33

Lucasville

Pinewood-T was standing at the front of his cell when a C.O. let J-Bo out for his visit.

"Have a good one, my baby," he called out through the bars.

"For sho', bro," J-Bo replied, as he strode past.

As he was leaving the block, a porter carried a mop bucket up to the second range and began mopping. He stopped at Pinewood-T's cell and held a brief conversation.

"You understand if I give you this, you gotta use it, right?" said the porter, who was a high-ranking member of the Aryan Brotherhood.

"Trust me," Pinewood-T replied with a cold stare. "If you hold up yo' end, I'm definitely gon' hold up mines."

Without another word, the porter reached down into the bucket of water, grabbed a foot-long sword and swiftly slipped it between the bars. "Be on the door at a quarter after," he said before walking off.

Drying off the knife, Pinewood-T inspected its sharpness before hiding it inside his mattress. This was what he would use on an unsuspecting J-Bo when he returned from his visit.

It was a week ago when Pinewood-T and J-Bo were talking and he suddenly remembered where he recognized J-Bo's voice from. This the bitch ass nigga that shot me, he said to himself, heatedly recalling the robbery he barely survived.

Forced to walk with a permanent limp on account of J-Bo, revenge was not something Pinewood-T could deny himself. So for a $500 Cash-App, he was given the knife and assurance that his door would be popped when J-Bo returned from his visit.

Psyching himself up to possibly catch a body, Pinewood-T had his fellow Detroit native 'Tee Grizzley' on repeat.

"I don't sleep on no beef (naw)/You know I'm on top of everythin', nigga

I come on yo' street (yeah)/Fuck talkin' let that metal bang

I don't squash no beef (naw)/We ain't doing no flex/ I was taught to handle everythin'...

I don't play wit' no beef (naw)/Run in his crib an' kill everything livin'."

***

Winton Terrace . . .

Inside a plushed out apartment on Craft, Shake-D and Tilla were hurriedly packing money and personal belongings into a suitcase. After laying low since the night of D-Wub's arrest, paranoia had convinced them to get out of town. So earlier that morning, Shake-D bought two train tickets to another state.

After peeking out the blinds for any unfamiliar vehicles, they nervously exited the apartment and hopped inside a '93 Toyota.

"I think you should get in the backseat," Tilla told Shake-D before pulling off. "It'll look less suspicious if I gotta go pass a cop car."

His point plausible, Shake-D wordlessly climbed into the backseat and lay down.

Noticing nothing strange as he drove down Winneste, Tilla turned onto Kings Run and was suddenly cut off by a maroon Regal. When he slammed on the brakes and tried to throw the car in reverse, a masked man came out the sunroof with a fully-auto Glock-18.

Po-po-po-po-po-po-po-po-po-po-po-po-po-po-po-po!

Tilla never stood a chance as full metal jackets jammed into him from the jaw down.

As the Regal peeled out, the gunman let off another volley of shots before sliding back down into the car.

When the bullet-riddled Toyota coasted into a curb and stopped, Shake-D miraculously rose up from the backseat like Lazarus. With no time to mourn the loss of his comrade, who was the only reason he survived, he grabbed his suitcase and got missing. He still had a train to catch.

***

Twelve minutes later . . .

In the infamous hood known as 'Avondale', the maroon Regal made a right turn on Hale and parked in the middle of the block.

With their ski masks now rolled up into toboggans, Benny and Hobo hopped out the car and wordlessly marched around the corner to a duck-off on Carplin.

As Hiram's successor, Benny felt there were certain obligations that came along with inheriting the throne, and revenge was one of them. So after offering his condolences and $85,000 to Hiram's baby's mother, he assured her he would personally punish the people responsible for his death. "Before it's all said and done, I promise you," he said to her, "they gon' pay for what they did."

With everything falling perfectly into place, Benny would soon make a move that would enable him to checkmate his opponent with the simple push of a pawn.

Chapter 34

Lucasville

Inside the visiting room, J-Bo was unusually quiet as he slowly chewed on a chicken sandwich. Having paid little attention to Booka since he sat down, Heaven knew something must've really bothering him.

"I gotta use the bathroom," Booka softly announced to Heaven, after drinking his third bottle of apple juice. Still affected by the absence of his mother, he too was in a somber mood.

When they returned from the restroom, Heaven sat with J-Bo a few minutes longer before saying maybe it was best they leave. "Because you're obviously not ready to discuss whatever's bothering you, and this is not good energy for either of us."

His head down, J-Bo just nodded.

Giving Booka a hug and Heaven a brief kiss, J-Bo said he would try to call later and walked away. If he had turned around before entering the strip search room, he would've seen Heaven speaking with the officer at the front desk.

After performing the degrading ritual of nakedly squatting and coughing, J-Bo was putting his clothes back on when the phone rang.

"Officer Glover," the C.O. said into the receiver. As he was listening to the caller on the other end, a Shift Commander and two C.O.'s entered the room.

"Mr. Bowden, I'ma need you to face the wall," said the Shift Commander, who wore a starched white shirt and polished shoes.

"What's the problem, Serg'?" J-Bo inquired.

"Your loved ones seem to think you may be battling with a case of depression. And in light of your situation, I reviewed the cameras and noticed you did appear to be a bit spaced out during your visit. So for everyone's safety, we're just gonna place you in an observation room for a day or two."

"Come on, Serg'," J-Bo said in protest. "I promise you, I'm good. I just—"

"Just shut the fuck up and face the wall!" one of the C.O.'s barked as he stepped forward and clicked open his cuffs. "If you wonna kill your fucking self, then do that shit on another shift."

Stripped naked again and forced to wear a knee-length vest made of nylon, J-Bo was locked in a suicide-watch cell with a wool blanket and no sheets. Along with the eyes of a C.O., his movements would be monitored by a mounted camera set up in front of his cell.

It was during third shift when the officer looked up and noticed J-Bo in his cell having what appeared to be a heart attack.

"What's going on in there?" he yelled, jumping up from the desk.

Gasping for breath as he clutched at his chest, J-Bo staggered the front of the cell with a terrified expression. Slowly sinking to his knees, he fell sideways and lay still.

When medical arrived at his cell minutes later and checked his vitals, one of the nurses yelled in panic, "His blood pressure's ninety-over-fifty. Someone call an ambulance!"

Ten minutes later the paramedics had J-Bo on a stretcher, rushing him out to the ambulance. For security reasons, an armed officer rode up front, while two more trailed in a white van.

As they were travelling down the darkened highway, the driver of the van glanced in the rearview and saw headlights rapidly approaching. Before he could alert his partner, a pair of Yamaha 1000R's pulled alongside them, one of which was ridden by two people.

Communicating through Bluetooth equipped helmets, the rider on the back of the bike removed an AR Pistol from inside his leather racing jacket and sprayed the van with 223's. When it veered off the road and tumbled into a cornfield, both bikes then roared toward the ambulance, with dragon spit shooting out the titanium tailpipes.

When they got in front of the ambulance, the rider on the back daringly spun around until he was facing it, then motioned with the AR for them to pull over.

The father of a newborn with a beautiful wife, the C.O. riding shotgun in the ambulance ordered the driver to comply. Because not only was help on the way, but he was unwilling to risk his life for an inmate.

As the AR holder held the driver and C.O. at bay, the other two ran to the back of the ambulance and snatched open its doors.

Instructed not to cause casualties unless necessary, Graveyard pointed a hammerless .45 at one of the paramedics, then at the handcuffs on J-Bo's leg. "Tek it off!" he barked through the helmet.

"I don't have a key!" the man cried in fear.

Graveyard shot him, then turned the gun on the female paramedic, who hurriedly fetched the key from the C.O. up front. With trembling hands, she unlocked the cuffs and backed up.

Suddenly alive with energy as he tore the nasal cannula off his face, J-Bo hopped out the ambulance and ran to climb on back of a bike with Graveyard.

Poka-poka-poka-poka-poka-poka-poka!

Graveyard shot out the ambulance's front tires, then popped the clutch and roared off into the night; the prison break carried out in less than ten minutes.

J-Bo's heart attack had been a hoax. And so had the somber mood during the visit.

Also playing her role well was Heaven. Having removed a balloon from beneath her breasts when she took Booka to the bathroom, she slipped it to J-Bo during their brief kiss at the end of the visit. Then, to ensure he was somewhere he would receive immediate medical attention, she told the officer in the visiting room that she feared her boyfriend was suicidal.

When placed on suicide watch, J-Bo had anxiously laid under the blanket with his eyes periodically peering at the clock outside the cell. Then, minutes before both hands met at twelve, he reached inside his mouth and removed the small balloon that contained a Beta Blocker.

A pill that would drastically slow the beating of his heart, J-Bo prayed that all went well, then swallowed it and commenced to having a heart attack.

***

With his arms enclosed around Graveyard as they zipped down the highway at 140 mph, J-Bo couldn't believe he was actually a free man. Within minutes he had gone from doing a life sentence at a level-4 prison to breathing fresh air in the outside world.

And I ain't never going back, he vowed to himself, as he basked in the euphoric feeling of freedom. *I'd rather be carried by six.*

The crotch rockets turned off the highway and rolled into a small barn. Parking beside an idling hearse, Graveyard led J-Bo over to it and had him lay inside one of the two empty caskets.

As Graveyard and his men were hastily removing their racing gear, he raised his .45 and shot them both in the head.

After changing into a three-piece suit, Graveyard doused everything in gasoline, including the twenty-thousand-dollar bikes, then climbed behind the wheel of the hearse and threw it in reverse. While backing out, he tossed a lit match out the window and exited the barn as it went up in flames.

Headed to a private airstrip in Chillicothe, Ohio, the Jamaican gangster was less than an hour away from collecting a quarter million.

According to G.P.S., Graveyard was only three miles from his destination when he encountered a situation he had been praying to avoid—a roadblock. Over thirty miles from the initial crime scene, he had not expected the police to be out this far. But it was too late to turn around.

Cursing in his native tongue, he mentally prepared himself to handle the situation accordingly, and without fear. If death be his destiny, then so be it.

As he brought the hearse to a stop, two Highway Patrolmen approached his window. With their hands cautiously lingering near their holsters, one of them held a recent photo of J-Bo that showed his face from all angles.

Once they checked his credentials and established he was not the suspect, the patrolman showed him J-Bo's picture.

"Have you seen this man?"

Graveyard shook his head, "No suh."

He then questioned Graveyard in regards to him being on the road at this time of the night.

In a calm voice he explained that he was on his way to pick up two bodies from a mortuary in Chillicothe and return them to West Virginia.

The patrolman glared at Graveyard as he considered his answer, then stepped back and told him to exit the hearse.

Feigning fear, Graveyard replied, "Me uh want no troubles.''

"Neither do we," he stated, "Now please step out of the vehicle, sir."

With only a split second to make a decision, Graveyard relied on intuition and stepped out; the .45 holstered under his jacket.

Using L.E.D. flashlights to inspect the hearse's interior, the officers then made their way around back and opened the door. When one of them aimed his weapon at the coffins and ordered the other to open the lids, Graveyard's hand began creeping toward the .45 Colt.

After nervously opening the first coffin, which was empty, the officer then turned to the one beside it and slowly lifted its lid. He exhaled in relief when he saw that it, too, was empty.

Apologizing for the inconvenience, the patrolmen told Graveyard to have a good day, then radioed for him to be let through the roadblock.

Grateful for maintaining his composure, Graveyard threw his head back and laughed while continuing toward the airstrip.

"Me gonna be king uh Jamaica!"

Chapter 35

Chillicothe, Ohio

With exhaust softly exhaling from its tailpipes, an English White Range was parked inside the hangar when Graveyard pulled in. Behind the Rover's tinted windows sat Terry Jones and Fat-Cat, who were equally responsible for J-Bo's newfound freedom.

Terry Jones had begun arranging the pieces to J-Bo's escape shortly after finding about Booka. Because not only did the young lad need a father figure, but Terry knew he owed down for his failures and neglect of J-Bo, and was willing to repay him in whatever ways possible.

Terry Jones and Fat-Cat emerged from the truck as Graveyard went around to the back of the hearse.

Opening the lid of the second coffin, Graveyard pressed a secret latch beneath one of its handles, then reached inside to lift the undercarriage.

"Yuh free, rude bwoy!" he said to J-Bo, as he grabbed his hand and helped him climb out.

Still wearing the nylon vest, J-Bo smiled at Fat-Cat, who had been the final piece to his escape.

"Can't no words express my gratitude," J-Bo said before hugging him like he would a biological brother.

Turning to Terry with a solemn expression, J-Bo extended his hand and said, "I wouldn't be a man if I didn't say thank you for everything you've done over the years. Because regardless of how I feel, none of this would be possible without you."

Terry Jones nodded, desperately wanting to inform him of their kinship, but afraid of rejection. *Maybe one day*, he told himself for the thousandth time.

Once J-Bo exchanged the vest for a Ralph Lauren jogger outfit and dark shades, the four men piled inside the Range and drove out to the private jet that would fly J-Bo to another country.

After trading farewells for the last time, J-Bo exited the truck and walked up the plane's short flight of stairs. He paused at the top, turned to give a salute and disappeared inside.

Please let my boy be safe, Terry Jones silently prayed, as he watched the plane take off and ascend into the clouds.

As Fat-Cat steered them back to the airport in Columbus, he could now say he was officially done with the streets. Applying the advice of Kiona's father, he was withdrawing his loyalty from the streets and depositing it into his family.

The investment of a true boss!

Chapter 36

Butler County Jail

Separated by plexiglass, D-Wub and Lil' Perry were quietly conversing in regards to an heroin shipment scheduled to arrive the following day. Not wanting to ruin his reputation with the Asians, D-Wub needed business to continue as usual. Because despite facing a possible life sentence, he still had aspirations of one day reclaiming the throne.

Lucky to have not been included in the federal indictment, Lil' Perry had been faithfully coming to visit D-Wub since his arrest. Eagerly accepting the task of handling his personal affairs, he swore he would do whatever it took to prove his loyalty to the 'Pack.

"I'd rather lose my life than to let you down, 'Wub," Lil' Perry had told him during one of their initial visits. "So it would definitely be in yo' best interests to trust me."

Speaking in code, D-Wub gave him the location of the drop and another spot from where he would grab three million dollars, which was to be given to the deliverymen. "You gon' have to be bool, balm, and bollective on this one, Blood." D-Wub forewarned him. "Cause if they sense the slightest sign of fear or nervousness, it's gon' turn into a Old Western up in that bitch."

Savoring the tasteful flavors of fortune and fame, Lil' Perry had a whole different swag as he left the county jail. For tomorrow would mark the beginning of his hood supremacy.

Lil' Perry slid behind the wheel of a white 'Vette, looked at his passenger and smiled, "We rich."

Caressing his hands together in anticipation, Benny replied, "And who say chess can't be compared to real life."

Lil' Perry had switched sides shortly after D-Wub killed Booter. Secretly enraged behind the senseless killing of his best friend, the seed of revenge had been planted that night as he pushed his body into the Ohio River.

Using Hiram's death as a means to befriend Benny, Lil' Perry had approached him at Kenwood mall one weekend and said he knew what happened to his comrade, whose remains were yet to be located.

Benny had initially been skeptical of Lil' Perry. But after hearing him out, he realized the man had only one motive— revenge. Then, thinking several moves ahead like a chess master, Benny offered Lil' Perry a slot on the team under one condition; that he not make a move on D-Wub until he said so.

The time to move would occur when D-Wub and his inner circle got indicted. "Start going to visit that nigga," Benny had advised Lil' Perry. "Cause he gon' need a nigga to drive for him right now." True enough, after playing his position for the past month, Lil' Perry had just been crowned king of the city.

While listening to Lil' Perry as he spoke on the heroin shipment, Benny congratulated himself on being patient. For not jumping the gun, he was to be rewarded with something more valuable than D-Wub's life—his fortune.

As Lil' Perry was driving up Vine, he glanced in his rearview for the tenth time and swore they were being followed by a dark-colored SUV. Unsure if it was jack boys or Task Force, he alerted Benny of his suspicions.

"Turn on the next street and park," Benny said, as he reached beneath his seat and grabbed a Glock-48.

Making a right on Forest, Lil' Perry parked between two cars and killed the lights. When he checked his side mirror and saw the SUV bend the corner, he nervously turned back to Benny.

Bang!

The first shot Benny fired hit Lil' Perry in the cheek and knocked his head back into the driver side window.

"How the opps gon' join the opps?" Benny stated before he put two more in Lil' Perry's head.

Calmly climbing out the 'Vette, Benny went around the front of it and jumped up in the dark colored SUV that had been following them.

As Hobo pulled off, Benny looked at him and said, "Checkmate."

Chapter 37

Three months later

Lebanon

In solitary confinement for the assault of another inmate, Ghost was drenched in sweat as he shadow-boxed with an imaginary opponent. He pivoted left, threw a crisp six-punch combo, then jabbed his way out. Perceiving prison a battlefield that required the constant honing of skills, he was in the fifth round of a Super Middleweight Bout.

Unable to attend the funeral, Ghost's mother had recently succumbed to her sickness. Then, as if life couldn't worsen, the Wolf Pack got indicted; scissoring off his only means of outside support. Consumed with bitterness behind the bleakness of his situation, the young villain vented the only way he knew how—through acts of violence.

Ghost was in the middle of the seventh round when a porter slid an envelope beneath his door, knocked twice, and kept it moving.

Toweling off his face and hands before picking up the envelope, Ghost tore it open and smiled at the contents inside. There were several pictures of a nude woman, a joint of weed, and a message that read: Blood Gang 4 Life!

His spirits momentarily lifted, Ghost went to the door and *soo-woo'd* loud enough for the entire hole to hear.

Loyalty was no doubt the reason behind Ghost's currently serving a life sentence. And it was unfortunate that he had handed his unconditional loyalty to a man incapable of returning the gesture. But at the same time, the lawlessness of his lifestyle would've eventually earned him a bus ride to prison, which is proven through the number of incarcerated gang members.

So while Ghost would always harbor resentment toward D-Wub for abandoning him, it was actually his own choices that led to him watching life from the sideline.

Chapter 38

Butler County Jail

After Lil' Perry's murder and the interception of the heroin shipment, the Wolf Pack were struck by an even more crippling blow when they received their 'Discovery Motions'. September had indeed turned state. And she was nowhere to be found.

In exchange for immunity and witness protection, September gave detailed accounts of nearly every shipment received and murder committed over the past three years. The evidence was so incriminating that their lawyers said they would have to take whatever plea deal the prosecutor proposed.

Joe-Joe and Smoke were offered twenty years, while D-Wub was given the 'Leadership Role' and offered thirty.

With only a week to inform the prosecutor of their decision, the three men were currently congregated in Joe-Joe's cell.

"We clearly can't afford to go to trial and lose," Joe-Joe reasoned, looking from D-Wub to Smoke. "We'd have our appeal rights, but why risk the chance of never comin' home if we ain't got to?"

While neither man wanted to come home in their forty's or fifty's, Joe-Joe said that it was better than coming home in a pine box.

They were quietly entertaining their own stressful thoughts when several C.O.'s entered the block and yelled for everyone to lock down.

From the windows of their cells, Joe-Joe and Smoke curiously watched as the C.O.'s marched over to D-Wub's cell and popped his door.

"Step out and face the wall," one of them ordered, as he held a can of mace in a threatening manner.

After a search of his room, one of the C.O.'s came out carefully holding a razor blade between his index finger and thumb. "Found this inside a book."

The third C.O. removed his handcuffs and told D-Wub to place his hands behind his back.

Knowing the razor wasn't his, but also knowing it was pointless to say otherwise, D-Wub wordlessly complied.

"Call my lawyer!" he told Joe-Joe, who was staring out the window.

Joe-Joe nodded, unsure of what to think at this point.

Escorted to an isolation unit, D-Wub was placed in a single-man cell and told he would be seen by a disciplinary officer within several days.

"Until then, try to find God or something," one of the C.O.'s joked before they slammed the door and walked off.

Later that night, a C.O. was doing his rounds when he stopped at D-Wub's cell and looked in. Tapping his flashlight on the window, he asked, "Why is your bed unmade?"

Lying in a perfectly-made bed, D-Wub waved him off in irritation. "Get yo' bitch ass on somewhere!"

"I'm giving you a direct order to make up your bed," the C.O. said.

Reading a book by the author Kweli, D-Wub ignored him.

The C.O. continued to stand there for a minute, then left.

Thirty minutes later the C.O. was doing another round when he looked in D-Wub's cell and jumped back in shock. "Oh shit!" he cursed before running out the pod.

Returning a minute later with two more C.O.'s, they opened the door and rushed in.

When D-Wub jumped up, one of the C.O.'s crippled him with a punch to his kidneys, then put him in a rear-naked chokehold. While he was being to put to sleep, another C.O. was stripping the covers off his bed.

Held up in the air by one of the C.O.'s, D-Wub awakened to a nightmare. With the end of a sheet tied around his neck and his hands cuffed behind his back, they were tying the other end of the sheet around a light fixture. Fearfully realizing what was about to happen, he attempted to yell for help and the C.O. let him go; his oxygen supply instantly cut off as he dangled in midair.

Violently gagging, D-Wub now understood why they had told him to find God earlier. This whole thing had been planned, beginning with the razor blade.

After checking his pulse to be certain he was dead, they removed the handcuffs and cut the sheet.

"We tried to get in here and save him," joked one of the C.O.'s, who then radioed in a signal-three, which meant there was a medical emergency.

D-Wub's death had been at the request of the Asians. When he failed to establish contact after not paying for the last shipment, they had his name ran through a database and learned he was in federal custody. Refusing to run any unnecessary risks, arrangements were made to have him silenced before his next court date.

Upon receiving confirmation of the kill, Mr. Lee disconnected the call and reasoned to himself, "*What's a million dollars compared to the prevention of a federal indictment?*"

Chapter 39

Minneapolis, Minnesota

A red Jeep Compass pulled into 'Deluxe Detailing' and parked by its front entrance. Emerging from the vehicle in gray leggings and a U.M. T-shirt was a voluptuous brunette, whose heart-shaped bottom bounced hypnotically as she strode into the shop.

Approaching the front counter, where an employee stood behind it reviewing paperwork, she flashed a bright smile and said, "Hi, I was wondering what type of cleaning packages you have. My car desperately needs it."

Taking in the splash of freckles beneath her violet-colored eyes, Boss flirtatiously replied, "Well, for someone as pretty as you I'd recommend the Deluxe package, which includes the interior, exterior, and even the trunk."

"Wow. And can this happen today?"

Boss shrugged, "That depends on you."

"What do you mean?"

"Ain't you a student over at the university?"

"I am."

"Well, if you promise to recommend this shop to everyone you know, then not only will I throw in a discount, but I'll personally make sure your car looks as if it came fresh off a car lot."

In a playful way, she gave him a suspicious look and asked, "And exactly how can you guarantee all this?"

Boss came from behind the counter and answered, "Cause I'm the owner."

After wisely walking away from the Wolf Pack, Boss had migrated to Minnesota and began living the life of a law abiding citizen. In a city that overflowed with opportunities, he met and impregnated a beautiful woman shortly after opening up his auto detailing shop. Grateful for deciding to give himself a chance, the soldier now fought for a different cause—the wellbeing of he and his family.

As Boss was locking up the shop that night, he got a text from his girl asking him to pick up some Butter Pecan ice cream. *It's eleven at night*, he smiled to himself while texting her back that he would.

Boss was reaching for his car door handle when he felt a presence behind him and turned. He couldn't believe his eyes.

"Damn, homie, you look like you seen a ghost," Shake-D smirked, his hands stuffed inside his coat pockets.

Boss half-smiled. "Nah, kid, I'm just surprised to see you, that's all. This a long-ass way from the 'Nati."

Looking over his shoulders as if he was expecting sirens at any second, Shake-D suggested they go grab a drink. "I gotta lot to fill you in on," he said, walking around to the passenger side of Boss' pickup truck. "You know 'Wub an' nem got indicted."

His mind racing as he climbed behind the wheel, Boss was thinking of the best way to kill Shake-D, and where to dispose of the body. He had slaved too hard to deaden his past and would prevent it from being resurrected by any means necessary.

Chapter 40

Atlanta

Nearly a hundred people were in attendance as Terry Jones and Regina exchanged marriage vows. For the first time since being scarred by Simone, Terry was handing his heart to another woman. But after several years of their getting to know each other, he was certain Regina was who he would spend the rest of his life with.

". . . By the power vested into me, I now pronounce you husband and wife. You may kiss the bride."

When the two engaged in a passionate kiss, someone in the crowd yelled out, "A'ight now, we got children in here," which drew laughter among the crowd.

As they were walking down the aisle, with Regina proudly showcasing her nugget-size ring, Terry stopped to shake the hand of someone he'd grown quite fond of.

"I appreciate you showing up."

"And I appreciate the invitation," Fat-Cat replied, as he held hands with Kiona. Her stomach now the size of a watermelon, she was expected to be delivered of a baby girl in three weeks, whom they were naming Gianna "Gi-Gi'' Scott in memory of the legendary Kobe Bryant's daughter.

No longer shouldering the risks and responsibilities that were attached to the streets, Fat-Cat had never felt more alive in his entire life. Instead of finding joy from his involvements with the fast life, he now found joy in knowing that he would be present for 'Daddy/Daughter dances', graduation day, and every other significant event in his daughter's life.

After encouraging Fat-Cat to keep his sights on the stars, Terry Jones grabbed his wife's hand and led her outside to a chauffeured Bentley Bentayga, where they climbed into its backseat and rode off into the sunset.

Chapter 41

A Dodge Magnum, hauling three merciless mercenaries, marched into Magic City and braked right at the front entrance. Two of the ski-masked men exited the wagon with 50-round Glocks and no conscious.

In Nike tracksuits and ACG boots, the taller of the two raised his cannon and shot the doorman in the face. As the crowd fearfully fled, the two killers stepped over the body and proceeded into the club.

Inside the small establishment, the taller one shot several more security guards, as his comrade blew down on a man seated at a VIP stage table. Dripping in VVS's from ears to fingers, his eyes widened right before he was shot six times in the face and chest.

Amid the chaotic scene of screaming and scrambling, the two killers were backpedalling out the club when the manager rose up from behind the bar and opened fire.

Boom!-Boom!-Boom!-Boom!-Boom!-Boom!

As the taller killer collapsed from a hollow to his neck, his comrade promptly returned fire.

Pow! Pow! Pow! Pow! Pow! Pow! Pow!

Continuing to squeeze as he courageously advanced toward the manager, he leaned over the bar and dumped three R.I.P. rounds into the crown of his head. He then strode over to his critically-wounded accomplice and ended his suffering.

Pow! Pow!

Waving his gun from side-to-side as he moved toward the door, he let off several warning shots before turning to run back to the wagon. He lost no time in screeching away.

***

"What can make a nigga wanna go an' get it? /Said he want a beamer wit' the subs in it/ Said he grew up in a house an' it was love missin'/ Said he grew up in the set he keep his guns wit' him."

-Young Nigga

Vibing to Nipsey Hussle as he sat in the driver seat of a BMW 760i, Shooter was parked behind an abandoned building when the Dodge Magnum pulled in beside him.

After wiping down the interior and leaving the keys in the ignition, Blueface and Pig joined Shooter in the Beamer, which he threw in drive without a word being spoken.

A more ruthless boss than Fat-Cat, Shooter had sanctioned the hit on the man inside the club simply because he was a competitor in the pill business. Now, as a result of his earthly departure, his profits stood to double.

Like so many others who were obsessed with the practices of the street life, Shooter had no desire to depart from something that would one day desert him in a desolate place; whether it be above or below.

But maybe he already knew and was willing to accept his future forecast. Or maybe he didn't.

Maybe one day the true meaning of life he'll grasp . . . or maybe he won't.

Chapter 42

Bora Bora

Located in the middle of the Pacific Ocean, Bora Bora is French-speaking island surrounded by aquamarine-colored water. Its scenery consisting of palm trees, mountains, and modest homes, the true beauty of it is indescribable.

Inside one of the houses—which are elevated over shallow streams of water—a Smart TV showed the image of a woman who was giving a tutorial on how to speak French. And paying close attention was J-Bo, Heaven, and Booka.

Bora Bora had been J-Bo's idea. And for precautionary reasons, not even Terry Jones or Heaven's mother knew their exact location. They couldn't tell what they didn't know. However, Terry did mention that arrangements could be made if the need to relocate ever arose.

After watching the French-speaking DVD and practising the words they had just learned, Heaven put Booka in his room for a nap and joined J-Bo on the couch.

"A dollar for your thoughts," she said, hugging up on him.

"Nah, I'm just thinking how one minute life can be all good, and you can be cruisin' up Joyful Boulevard. Then one wrong turn, and the next thing you know, you stuck in a traffic jam on Hopeless Avenue. And as you sittin' there, certain you gon' miss out on every important event to which you were headed, a lane suddenly opens up and now you speeding down Revival Road."

J-Bo told Heaven that was how he saw the course of his life. One minute he was on earth enjoying himself, then in the blink of an eye he was hurled into hell with a heavy heart and no hope.

"The possibility of regaining my freedom seemed so far-fetched that I couldn't even picture myself being in the outside world no more. I continued to crawl, only because survival is all I know. But on the inside I was hurtin' so bad, and there was nobody to cry out to for help or latch onto for support."

"Then you and Booka showed up and saved me," J-Bo said, kissing her on the forehead. "And now here I am, suddenly living in this heavenly-like state of being."

"Do you know why that lane opened up for you, Javonte?"

"Why?"

"Because you deserve it. You're a genuine person at heart. And despite of all you've been through in life, you never allowed it to convert you into a monster. So I believe this is your way of being given a second chance."

"And you know what else?" Heaven said with a big smile.

"What?"

"I think Booka might be ready for a sibling."

J-Bo frowned, then the reality of her statement dawned on him and his eyes brightened with excitement. "You serious?"

Heaven nodded. "I think so. I'm never late, and it's been over a month."

After kissing her all over her face, J-Bo said he should go buy a pregnancy test from the store.

"Javonte," Heaven called out, as he opened the door to leave.

When he looked over his shoulder, she said, "I think you'll make a good father."

"I'm glad you think so," J-Bo smiled, then turned to leave and suddenly saw something that made his heart drop. *This can't be real*, he told himself in disbelief.

Standing before J-Bo with an operable and fully loaded firearm was Olivia's father, Dr. Patterson.

"Step back inside the house," Dr. Patterson ordered him in a calm but callous tone.

Glad that Booka was in his room, J-Bo slowly complied.

"Oh my god!" Heaven fearfully cried out before placing a hand over her mouth.

Protectively shielding her with his body, J-Bo couldn't believe this was happening. He had imagined many different scenarios in which things could go wrong, but this was something he would've never expected.

Closing the door behind himself, Dr. Patterson leveled the gun at J-Bo's chest and said, "This is the last time I'll ask you . . . where is my daughter?"

***

When Dr. Patterson learned of J-Bo's escape, his thoughts were consumed by a single word—closure. It was the only thing that prevented him from fully focusing on the progression of his life. So he approached God in prayer and asked for His hand in helping him track down a man that not even law enforcement could locate.

"Lord, I know I'm about to embark on a journey that you may or not approve of. But you know how desperate I am in finding my little girl. So I ask that you please allow me to bring her home."

It would be two months before his prayer was answered. *Thank you, Lord*, he prayed in gratitude, then took a leave of absence from work and booked a flight to the island.

As Dr. Patterson held J-Bo at gunpoint, he could see the wheels in his mind turning and took a step closer.

"Please, don't make me become someone I'm not," he warned, tightening his grip on the gun. "All I'm asking you to do is tell me where she is."

When Heaven set aside her fear and really observed Dr. Patterson, she was able to sense two things; he was not prone to violence, but would do whatever it took to acquire the closure for which he'd come. In spite of the present danger her and J-Bo were facing, she couldn't help but wish she had been conceived by a father as loyal and dedicated as Olivia's.

Partly aware of what Dr. Patterson was referring to, she squeezed J-Bo's hand, silently urging him to grant the man's request. He had suffered long enough.

Dr. Patterson noticed her gesture and quickly cut in, "Please, young man. I'm not here to turn you in or cause you any grief. As the Lord is my witness, I only wish to give my little girl a decent burial."

Heaven caught J-Bo's eye and gave him a subtle nod. It was time to move on.

After years of maintaining his silence in regards to Olivia's death and disappearance, J-Bo revealed the location of her skeletal remains. And it was so shocking that Dr. Patterson couldn't believe his ears. She was somewhere no one would've ever thought to look—in the same cemetery as her mother.

On behalf of his wife's dying wishes, Dr. Patterson had purchased three burial plots at 'Resting In Peace' cemetery. The plots side-by-side, his wife said that when their inevitable times arrived, she wanted them to be in the same place. "I'm not expecting to see you or Livy anytime soon," she had said during her final hours, "but when the day does come, I would just like for us to all be together."

A pair of tears rolled down Dr. Patterson's cheeks as he regarded J-Bo with a somewhat appreciative expression. While he most certainly had no right to claim his daughter's life, at least he had had the love and decency to bury her where she rightfully belonged.

"How did you know?" J-Bo asked out of curiosity, as Dr. Patterson turned to leave.

With his hand on the doorknob, he paused to answer him without looking back. "This was where Olivia wanted to live one day."

Chapter 43

Sri Lanka

With Booka settled on top of his shoulders, J-Bo and Heaven held hands as the three strolled down the darkened beach.

". . . And if it's a boy," J-Bo smiled, "then you already know we gotta name him Kobe De'Juan Bowden."

After the intrusion of Dr. Patterson, J-Bo knew the risk of remaining in Bora Bora was too great, regardless of him swearing not to mention their location to anyone. So he took Terry Jones up on his offer and relocated to Sri Lanka, which was on the southern tip of India.

As they were walking back home later that night, Heaven glanced at J-Bo, who had suddenly grown quiet.

"What's on your mind?" she inquired, squeezing his hand affectionately.

"Sometimes I just be wondering if I'm being selfish or asking too much of you. Because you know being with me means you probably won't get to see your loved ones for a long time. And I just don't want you to end up resenting me one day."

"I could *never* resent you, Javonte," Heaven immediately replied. "So if being with you means the sacrifice of my family . . ." she looked up at him and shrugged, "then I guess it's just *the cost of loyalty*."

The End…

Submission Guideline

Submit the first three chapters of your completed manuscript to ldpsubmissions@gmail.com, subject line: Your book's title. The manuscript must be in a .doc file and sent as an attachment. Document should be in Times New Roman, double spaced and in size 12 font. Also, provide your synopsis and full contact information. If sending multiple submissions, they must each be in a separate email.

Have a story but no way to send it electronically? You can still submit to LDP/Ca$h Presents. Send in the first three chapters, written or typed, of your completed manuscript to:

LDP: Submissions Dept
Po Box 870494
Mesquite, Tx 75187

DO NOT send original manuscript. Must be a duplicate.

Provide your synopsis and a cover letter containing your full contact information.

Thanks for considering LDP and Ca$h Presents.

Coming Soon from Lock Down Publications/Ca$h Presents

BOW DOWN TO MY GANGSTA

By **Ca$h**

TORN BETWEEN TWO

By **Coffee**

THE STREETS STAINED MY SOUL **II**

By **Marcellus Allen**

BLOOD OF A BOSS **VI**

SHADOWS OF THE GAME II

By **Askari**

LOYAL TO THE GAME **IV**

By **T.J. & Jelissa**

A DOPEBOY'S PRAYER **II**

By **Eddie "Wolf" Lee**

IF LOVING YOU IS WRONG… **III**

By **Jelissa**

TRUE SAVAGE **VII**

MIDNIGHT CARTEL III

DOPE BOY MAGIC III

By **Chris Green**

BLAST FOR ME **III**

A SAVAGE DOPEBOY III

CUTTHROAT MAFIA II

By **Ghost**

A HUSTLER'S DECEIT III

KILL ZONE **II**

BAE BELONGS TO ME III

By **Aryanna**

CHAINED TO THE STREETS III

By **J-Blunt**

KING OF NEW YORK V

COKE KINGS IV

BORN HEARTLESS IV

By **T.J. Edwards**

GORILLAZ IN THE BAY V

TEARS OF A GANGSTA II

De'Kari

THE STREETS ARE CALLING II

Duquie Wilson

KINGPIN KILLAZ IV

STREET KINGS III

PAID IN BLOOD III

CARTEL KILLAZ IV

DOPE GODS II

Hood Rich

SINS OF A HUSTLA II

ASAD

TRIGGADALE III

Elijah R. Freeman

KINGZ OF THE GAME V

Playa Ray

SLAUGHTER GANG IV

RUTHLESS HEART IV

By Willie Slaughter

THE HEART OF A SAVAGE III

By Jibril Williams

FUK SHYT II

By Blakk Diamond

THE DOPEMAN'S BODYGAURD II

By Tranay Adams

TRAP GOD II

By Troublesome

YAYO III

A SHOOTER'S AMBITION III

By S. Allen

GHOST MOB

Stilloan Robinson

KINGPIN DREAMS II

By Paper Boi Rari

CREAM

By Yolanda Moore

SON OF A DOPE FIEND II

By Renta

FOREVER GANGSTA II

GLOCKS ON SATIN SHEETS II

By Adrian Dulan

LOYALTY AIN'T PROMISED II

By Keith Williams

THE PRICE YOU PAY FOR LOVE II

DOPE GIRL MAGIC II

By Destiny Skai

THE LIFE OF A HOOD STAR

By Rashia Wilson

TOE TAGZ III

By Ah'Million

CONFESSIONS OF A GANGSTA II

By Nicholas Lock

PAID IN KARMA III

By **Meesha**

I'M NOTHING WITHOUT HIS LOVE II

By Monet Dragun

CAUGHT UP IN THE LIFE II

By Robert Baptiste

NEW TO THE GAME II

By **Malik D. Rice**

Life of a Savage II

By **Romell Tukes**

Quiet Money II

By **Trai'Quan**

THE STREETS MADE ME II

By **Larry D. Wright**

Available Now

RESTRAINING ORDER **I & II**

By **CA$H & Coffee**

LOVE KNOWS NO BOUNDARIES **I II & III**

By **Coffee**

RAISED AS A GOON I, II, III & IV

BRED BY THE SLUMS I, II, III

BLAST FOR ME I & II

ROTTEN TO THE CORE I II III

A BRONX TALE I, II, III

DUFFEL BAG CARTEL I II III IV

HEARTLESS GOON I II III IV

A SAVAGE DOPEBOY I II

HEARTLESS GOON I II III

DRUG LORDS I II III

CUTTHROAT MAFIA

By **Ghost**

LAY IT DOWN **I & II**

LAST OF A DYING BREED

BLOOD STAINS OF A SHOTTA I & II III

By **Jamaica**

LOYAL TO THE GAME I II III

LIFE OF SIN I, II III

By **TJ & Jelissa**

BLOODY COMMAS I & II

SKI MASK CARTEL I II & III

KING OF NEW YORK I II,III IV

RISE TO POWER I II III

COKE KINGS I II III

BORN HEARTLESS I II III

By **T.J. Edwards**

IF LOVING HIM IS WRONG…I & II

LOVE ME EVEN WHEN IT HURTS I II III

By **Jelissa**

WHEN THE STREETS CLAP BACK I & II III

THE HEART OF A SAVAGE I II

By **Jibril Williams**

A DISTINGUISHED THUG STOLE MY HEART I II & III

LOVE SHOULDN'T HURT I II III IV

RENEGADE BOYS I II III IV

PAID IN KARMA I II

By **Meesha**

A GANGSTER'S CODE I &, II III

A GANGSTER'S SYN I II III

THE SAVAGE LIFE I II III

CHAINED TO THE STREETS I II

By J-Blunt

PUSH IT TO THE LIMIT

By **Bre' Hayes**

BLOOD OF A BOSS **I, II, III, IV, V**

SHADOWS OF THE GAME

By **Askari**

THE STREETS BLEED MURDER **I, II & III**

THE HEART OF A GANGSTA I II& III

By **Jerry Jackson**

CUM FOR ME I II III IV V

An **LDP Erotica Collaboration**

BRIDE OF A HUSTLA **I II & II**

THE FETTI GIRLS **I, II& III**

CORRUPTED BY A GANGSTA I, II III, IV

BLINDED BY HIS LOVE

THE PRICE YOU PAY FOR LOVE

DOPE GIRL MAGIC

By **Destiny Skai**

WHEN A GOOD GIRL GOES BAD

By **Adrienne**

THE COST OF LOYALTY I II III

By Kweli

A GANGSTER'S REVENGE **I II III & IV**

THE BOSS MAN'S DAUGHTERS I II III IV V

A SAVAGE LOVE **I & II**

BAE BELONGS TO ME I II

A HUSTLER'S DECEIT I, II, III

WHAT BAD BITCHES DO I, II, III

SOUL OF A MONSTER I II III

KILL ZONE

By **Aryanna**

A KINGPIN'S AMBITON

A KINGPIN'S AMBITION **II**

I MURDER FOR THE DOUGH

By **Ambitious**

TRUE SAVAGE I II III IV V VI

DOPE BOY MAGIC I, II

MIDNIGHT CARTEL I II

By **Chris Green**

A DOPEBOY'S PRAYER

By **Eddie "Wolf" Lee**

THE KING CARTEL **I, II & III**

By **Frank Gresham**

THESE NIGGAS AIN'T LOYAL **I, II & III**

By **Nikki Tee**

GANGSTA SHYT **I II &III**

By **CATO**

THE ULTIMATE BETRAYAL

By **Phoenix**

BOSS'N UP **I , II & III**

By **Royal Nicole**

I LOVE YOU TO DEATH

By Destiny J

I RIDE FOR MY HITTA

I STILL RIDE FOR MY HITTA

By **Misty Holt**

LOVE & CHASIN' PAPER

By **Qay Crockett**

TO DIE IN VAIN

SINS OF A HUSTLA

By **ASAD**

BROOKLYN HUSTLAZ

By **Boogsy Morina**

BROOKLYN ON LOCK I & II

By **Sonovia**

GANGSTA CITY

By **Teddy Duke**

A DRUG KING AND HIS DIAMOND I & II III

A DOPEMAN'S RICHES

HER MAN, MINE'S TOO I, II

CASH MONEY HO'S

By Nicole Goosby

TRAPHOUSE KING **I II & III**

KINGPIN KILLAZ I II III

STREET KINGS I II

PAID IN BLOOD **I II**

CARTEL KILLAZ I II III

DOPE GODS

By **Hood Rich**

LIPSTICK KILLAH **I, II, III**

CRIME OF PASSION I II & III

By **Mimi**

STEADY MOBBN' **I, II, III**

THE STREETS STAINED MY SOUL

By **Marcellus Allen**

WHO SHOT YA **I, II, III**

SON OF A DOPE FIEND

Renta

GORILLAZ IN THE BAY **I II III IV**

TEARS OF A GANGSTA

DE'KARI

TRIGGADALE I II

Elijah R. Freeman

GOD BLESS THE TRAPPERS I, II, III

THESE SCANDALOUS STREETS I, II, III

FEAR MY GANGSTA I, II, III

THESE STREETS DON'T LOVE NOBODY I, II

BURY ME A G I, II, III, IV, V

A GANGSTA'S EMPIRE I, II, III, IV

THE DOPEMAN'S BODYGAURD

Tranay Adams

THE STREETS ARE CALLING

Duquie Wilson

MARRIED TO A BOSS… I II III

By Destiny Skai & Chris Green

KINGZ OF THE GAME I II III IV

Playa Ray

SLAUGHTER GANG I II III

RUTHLESS HEART I II III

By Willie Slaughter

FUK SHYT

By Blakk Diamond

DON'T F#CK WITH MY HEART I II

By Linnea

ADDICTED TO THE DRAMA I II III

By Jamila

YAYO I II

A SHOOTER'S AMBITION I II

By S. Allen

TRAP GOD

By Troublesome

FOREVER GANGSTA

GLOCKS ON SATIN SHEETS

By Adrian Dulan

TOE TAGZ I II

By Ah'Million

KINGPIN DREAMS

By Paper Boi Rari

CONFESSIONS OF A GANGSTA

By Nicholas Lock

I'M NOTHING WITHOUT HIS LOVE

By Monet Dragun

CAUGHT UP IN THE LIFE

By Robert Baptiste

NEW TO THE GAME

By **Malik D. Rice**

Life of a Savage

By **Romell Tukes**

LOYALTY AIN'T PROMISED

By Keith Williams

Quiet Money

By **Trai'Quan**

THE STREETS MADE ME

By **Larry D. Wright**

BOOKS BY LDP'S CEO, CA$H

TRUST IN NO MAN

TRUST IN NO MAN 2

TRUST IN NO MAN 3

BONDED BY BLOOD

SHORTY GOT A THUG

THUGS CRY

THUGS CRY 2

THUGS CRY 3

TRUST NO BITCH

TRUST NO BITCH 2

TRUST NO BITCH 3

TIL MY CASKET DROPS

RESTRAINING ORDER

RESTRAINING ORDER 2

IN LOVE WITH A CONVICT

Coming Soon

BONDED BY BLOOD 2

BOW DOWN TO MY GANGSTA

www.ingramcontent.com/pod-product-compliance
Lightning Source LLC
Chambersburg PA
CBHW070520260626
47161CB00004B/1596

9781951081959